AF812496

Palgrave Studies in Affect Theory and Literary Criticism

Series Editors

Adam Frank
University of British Columbia
Vancouver, British Columbia, Canada

Joel Faflak
Western University
London, Ontario, Canada

The recent surge of interest in affect and emotion has productively crossed disciplinary boundaries within and between the humanities, social sciences, and sciences, but has not often addressed questions of literature and literary criticism as such. The first of its kind, Palgrave Studies in Affect Theory and Literary Criticism seeks theoretically informed scholarship that examines the foundations and practice of literary criticism in relation to affect theory. This series aims to stage contemporary debates in the field, addressing topics such as: the role of affective experience in literary composition and reception, particularly in non-Western literatures; examinations of historical and conceptual relations between major and minor philosophies of emotion and literary experience; and studies of race, class, gender, sexuality, age, and disability that use affect theory as a primary critical tool.

More information about this series at
http://www.springer.com/series/14653

Jean-François Vernay

The Seduction of Fiction

A Plea for Putting Emotions Back into Literary Interpretation

Translated by Carolyne Lee

palgrave
macmillan

Jean-François Vernay
Noumea, New Caledonia

Translated by Carolyne Lee
The original edition of this translation was published by Complicités in Paris, in 2013, under the title: *Plaidoyer pour un renouveau de l'émotion en littérature*

Palgrave Studies in Affect Theory and Literary Criticism
ISBN 978-3-319-39452-7 ISBN 978-3-319-39453-4 (eBook)
DOI 10.1007/978-3-319-39453-4

Library of Congress Control Number: 2016950033

© The Editor(s) (if applicable) and The Author(s) 2016
This work is subject to copyright. All rights are solely and exclusively licensed by the Publisher, whether the whole or part of the material is concerned, specifically the rights of translation, reprinting, reuse of illustrations, recitation, broadcasting, reproduction on microfilms or in any other physical way, and transmission or information storage and retrieval, electronic adaptation, computer software, or by similar or dissimilar methodology now known or hereafter developed.
The use of general descriptive names, registered names, trademarks, service marks, etc. in this publication does not imply, even in the absence of a specific statement, that such names are exempt from the relevant protective laws and regulations and therefore free for general use.
The publisher, the authors and the editors are safe to assume that the advice and information in this book are believed to be true and accurate at the date of publication. Neither the publisher nor the authors or the editors give a warranty, express or implied, with respect to the material contained herein or for any errors or omissions that may have been made.

Cover illustration: © Melisa Hasan

Printed on acid-free paper

This Palgrave Macmillan imprint is published by Springer Nature
The registered company is Springer International Publishing AG Switzerland

Desire is the engine of life, the yearning that goads us forward with stops along the way, but it has no destination, no final stop, except death. The wondrous fullness after a meal or sex or a great book or conversation is inevitably short-lived. By nature, we want and we wish, and we assign content to that emptiness as we narrate our inner lives. For better and for worse, we bring meaning to it, one inevitably shaped by the language and culture in which we live. Meaning itself may be the ultimate human seduction.

Siri Hustvedt, "Variations on desire: a mouse, a dog, Buber and Bovary"

Author's Preface to the English Edition

When given the opportunity to express himself on the fate of literature, Jonathan Coe's character—Professor Leonard Davis, author of *The Failure of Contemporary Literature*—does not mince words:

> "The older one gets," said Davis, with his mouth full of cake, "the less useful critical theory seems."
> "You mean one should go back to texts?" asked Hugh.
> "Yes, perhaps. But then, the more one reads them, the less interesting the texts themselves appear to become."
> "This essentially is what you've been arguing in your new book," said Christopher. "It's a radical and provocative viewpoint, if I may so."
> Davis nodded his acquiescence.
> "But does this mean," Hugh asked carelessly, "the end of literature as we know it?"
> "As we know it?"
> "As it is taught in our schools and universities."
> "Ah! No, no … indeed not. Far from it. In fact I think—" here, there was an almighty pause, far surpassing any that had gone before "—I think …" Suddenly he looked up, the gleam of insight in his eye. The tension in the air was palpable. "I think I'd like another macaroon."[1]

Beyond the jocular note, this excerpt from *A Touch of Love* (1989) illustrates how the demise of literature and the uselessness of literary criticism regularly emerge as prime concerns in controversial debates. Completed in 2011, *Plaidoyer pour un renouveau de l'émotion en littérature* (Plea for a renewal of emotion in literature) was first published in 2013 in France, at a time when the community of French theorists and academics was publishing prolifically in order to sound alarm bells about students' peculiar estrangement from Literary Studies, to the point where the usefulness of academic courses and training over the last two decades was even called into question.[2]

To account for such an estrangement, Jérôme David[3] has listed three major stances:

1. Tzvetan Todorov puts it down to a kind of rigid formalism, essentially enshrined in schooling, whereby pupils are expected to be technical readers rather than passionate interpreters of fiction;
2. Jean-Marie Schaeffer feels that the evolution of literary studies over the last 20 years has generated a form of self-containment dictated by a set of fictional traits—such as the lack of extralinguistic referential properties or the absence of truth.[4] As a result, Schaeffer observes that literature has grown in isolation from other forms of discourse;
3. In line with reader-response theory, Yves Citton contends that students are being forced into a state of passive reading when they should be encouraged to become far more inquisitive about the texts under close scrutiny so as to form an "interpretive community" (Stanley Fish) of readers.

But my aim is not to discuss "the end of literature as we know it"; otherwise, I would have titled my book "A Farewell to Literature" as William Marx did.[5] My manifesto does not seek to mourn the causes of the alleged death of literature which, according to Marx, has been consistently self-proclaimed since the end of the nineteenth century. His view spanning three centuries of literary history and divided into three stages—namely expansion, autonomization, and devaluation—is self-explanatory enough not to need any further elaboration.

By articulating the three key components of literary interaction (i.e., the writing, reading, and interpreting processes), the wager of writing my book lay not so much in the capacity to take stock of the crisis sweeping through the beleaguered humanities, as in the ability to seek new directions and offer new tools that would do justice to the values of literature. Hence, my attempt at exposing the outline of what I call the psycholiterary approach. Another difficulty in the course of writing *Plaidoyer pour un renouveau de l'émotion en littérature* lay in the choice of words: "Fiction and literature are not synonymous,"[6] as Terry Eagleton boldly declares after he himself uses literature and fiction as interchangeable terms for a few chapters. Clearly, these words are not to be conflated but have nevertheless been used more or less synonymously in my original French edition for stylistic purposes. This is because authors who wish to write elegantly in French are tacitly expected not to repeat words within at least a couple of lines. This stylistic requirement can become an issue when words such as fiction and literature, though quasi-synonymous in meaning, are sensu stricto non-interchangeable concepts. In contrast, the translator of *The Seduction of Fiction: A Plea for Putting Emotions Back into Literary Interpretation,* Carolyne Lee, is able to use repetitions more freely in English, and has aptly taken the liberty to reinstate the most apposite concept wherever possible.

It is of utmost importance that we, human beings, whose emotional intelligence still gives us the edge on artificial intelligence, make good use of our advantage by exploring it to the full. In its 2010 benchmark statement defining the nationwide framework for senior high school teachers, the French Ministry of Education for once acknowledged the crucial role emotions play when reading fiction. As I have stated in a *Vox Poetica* interview,[7] even if the scientific approach to the humanities partakes of a need to objectify the assessment criteria within the educational sector, turning critical practice into some form of science will surely result in an asymptotic enterprise in which professional readers will systematically miss the goal, no matter how close they manage to get. And close enough will never be good enough. Clearly, the objectives of science and those of the humanities are as polar as those of the brain's left and right hemispheres: While the left hemisphere, like science, aims at thinking about our world as analytically and objectively as can be, the right—very much like the arts—favors a synthetic perspective based on intuition and emotions. The challenge is therefore to solve the paradox which aims at acknowledging and reinstating the subjectivity of reading practices by taking into account the plasticity of interpretation and its emotional aspects within secondary and tertiary education, systems that for the most part still require objective analyses.

Having said this, a great deal of European university-affiliated research centers and groups, having jumped on the "affective turn" bandwagon, are waking up to the interdisciplinary potentialities of investigating affective and cognitive sciences in the humanities. The Swiss Réseau Romand de Narratologie (federated under the twin aegis of the European Narratology Network and the International Society for the Study of Narrative), and the French Pouvoir des Arts project could be regarded as two telling examples of the fruitful interimplication of science and the arts. The three key components of literary interaction can largely benefit from the advance of neuroscience research which, someday, might well end up pinning down the much discussed singularity of literature through concepts such as mirror-neurons, brain plasticity, Theory of Mind (that is, the capacity to imagine and appreciate other people's mental states), the reconfiguration of memory, fantasizing, altered states of consciousness, embodied cognition, cognitive simulation, motor cognition, as-if body loops, and emotions like empathy. On another level, the study of emotions in fiction will emphasize the notion that writing is an embodied act whose corporeality is now the subject of many academic investigations through a range of buzz themes such as gesture, embodiment, body language, kinesia, just to name a few. Examined through a scientific lens, emotions will even confirm the argument that literary fiction has a shaping influence over readers, as tested by two teams of researchers from New York and Toronto.[8] Results of a study conducted by Emanuele Castano and David Comer Kidd, published in *Science* on 18 October 2013, concur with the view that reading literary fiction improves empathy, social perception, and emotional intelligence—albeit temporarily.

When considering fiction through the angle of seduction, literary theorists might as well ask themselves the right questions. Rather than pointlessly wondering who, nowadays, would still show an interest—let alone a vested one—in fiction, it might be more worthwhile addressing ways in which fiction could be of interest to contemporary readers. Psychologists and neuroscientists exploring the social values of literature through Theory of Mind may hold the key to this fairly new field of research, but literary theorists may also have a say in this matter. For Swiss scholar Yves Citton, who developed a few leads of his own in his 2007 book *Lire, interpréter, actualiser. Pourquoi les études littéraires?* (Read, interpret, actualize: why study literature?), studying literature is a means to cultivate one's tastes, to shape one's sensitivity, to guide one's love, and to reassess one's priorities and ends.[9]

While it seems timely to reinstate the usefulness and varied virtues of reading fiction, more important perhaps is to find ways in which fiction would be made more interesting to contemporary readers. *The Seduction of Fiction: A Plea for Putting Emotions Back into Literary Interpretation* specifically addresses these issues, among many others.

Noumea, New Caledonia
March 2016

Jean-François Vernay

Notes

1. Jonathan Coe, *A Touch of Love* (London: Penguin, 1989), 58.
2. See Dominique Maingueneau, *Contre Saint-Proust. La fin de la Littérature* (Paris: Belin, 2006); Yves Citton, *Lire, interpréter, actualiser. Pourquoi les études littéraires?* (Paris: Editions Amsterdam, 2007); Tzvetan Todorov, *La Littérature en péril* (Paris: Flammarion, 2007); Antoine Compagnon, *La littérature pour quoi faire?* (Paris: Fayard/Collège de France, 2007); Yves Citton, *L'avenir des humanités. Economie de la connaissance ou cultures de l'interprétation?* (Paris: La Découverte, 2010); Vincent Jouve, *Pourquoi étudier la littérature?* (Paris: Armand Colin, 2010); or Jean-Marie Schaeffer, *Petite écologie des études littéraires. Pourquoi et comment étudier la littérature?* (Paris: Thierry Marchaisse, 2011).
3. See Jérôme David, "Chloroforme et signification: Pourquoi la littérature est-elle si soporifique à l'école?", *Études de Lettres* 295, 2014/1, in Raphaël Baroni & Antonio Rodriguez (eds.), *Les passions en littérature. De la théorie à l'enseignement*, 19–32.
4. For a detailed discussion of heterorepresentation and truth-valuation, see Jean-François Vernay: "The Truth About Fiction as Possible Worlds," *Journal of Language, Literature and Culture* 61: 2, August 2014, 133–141.
5. William Marx, *L'Adieu à la littérature. Histoire d'une dévalorisation. XVIIIe–XXe siècle* (Paris: Les Editions de Minuit, 2005).
6. Terry Eagleton, *The Event of Literature* (New Haven/London: Yale University Press, 2012), 108.
7. Raphaël Baroni, "Retrouver les émotions dans les études littéraires," *Vox Poetica*, 01 February 2015. Accessed on 10, 14 April 2015: http://www.vox-poetica.org/entretiens/intVernay.html?fb_ref=Default.
8. See Castano, Emanuele, and David Comer Kidd. 2013. Reading Literary Fiction Improves Theory of Mind. *Science*, 342(6156): 377–380; and Maja Djikic & Keith Oatley, "The art in fiction: From indirect communication to changes of the self," *Psychology of Aesthetics, Creativity, and the Arts* 8: 4, Nov 2014, 498–505.
9. "... étudier la littérature, c'est un moyen de cultiver ses goûts, de façonner sa sensibilité, d'orienter ses amours, de réévaluer ses priorités et ses fins," Yves Citton, *Lire, interpréter, actualiser. Pourquoi les études littéraires?* (Paris: Editions Amsterdam, 2007), 156.

Translator's Note

The original French version of this book was published in 2013 in Paris, under the title *Plaidoyer pour un renouveau de l'émotion en littérature* (Plea for a renewal of emotion in literature). It was well received in France, with the author interviewed in the prestigious literary journal *vox-poetica*, and the book shortlisted for the French prize, *Le Prix Littéraire du Savoir et de la Recherche* (literary prize for knowledge and research), alongside books by Julia Kristeva and Alain Finkielkraut.

Jean-François Vernay outlines the cultural context of the original book in his author's preface, written in English especially for this edition. This was the only section of the book I did not translate, apart from some short quotations throughout the book from French authors, of which published English editions already existed; for quotations where published English editions do not exist, the translations are my own. The provenance of translations will be clear from their respective endnotes.

In his Preface, the author speaks of the condition of the "beleaguered humanities," a phenomenon known only too well in educational institutions in many parts of the English-speaking world. But what is not necessarily so well known are the French and European theorists closer to Vernay's own cultural situation, many of whom are not available in English. It is this synergy of known and unknown, of French/European and English/American/Australian traditions of scholarly criticism, that is so exciting about this book, that endows it with so much potential for intercultural insight. And it was in no small part for this reason that, from the moment I read the book in its original French, I felt an overwhelming desire to translate it.

But an equally important contribution to this desire was the book's argument for a new interdisciplinary approach, founded on advances in neuroscience, aiming to integrate psychology with literary analysis into the psycholiterary approach; in so doing, it opens up a space in which the formation of our emotions, our joys and sorrows, loves and hatreds, and everything in between, can be openly examined and discussed, potentially improving our capacities for empathy, social perception, and emotional intelligence. This book is thus one of a small but growing number of theoretical works aiming to incorporate scientific findings into the humanities, a move that could help to ameliorate the ongoing polarization of the two academic cultures, an amelioration called for in the mid-twentieth century by English scientist and novelist (and staunch defender of the novel) C. P. Snow. As Snow argued then, science "has got to be assimilated along with, and as part and parcel of, the whole of our mental experience."[1] With his psycholiterary approach, Jean-François Vernay is arguing for precisely this assimilation, as necessary now as it was in Snow's time, if not more so.

In all translations, certain changes are necessary, no matter how faithful one might wish to be to the original. Yet as Walter Benjamin has argued somewhat prescriptively, "a real translation … does not cover the original, does not block its light," but nevertheless must be rendered in language that "can—in fact, must—let itself go, so that it gives voice to the intention of the original not as reproduction but as harmony."[2]

Harmony has been an overriding goal for me in the translation of this book, since it is also a strong element in the original, but this goal has often been in tension with fidelity. It has been fortunate, then, that from the outset, the author and I were able to discuss a good many words and phrases in the translation, learning more about them and about our own practices of translation and/or language use as we did so. The book has benefitted immeasurably from this process. For, in common with the translator of the 20th English edition of *Madame Bovary* (Lydia Davis), Jean-François Vernay and I share the view that a translation, "one that is worth taking trouble over, is always a work in progress: it can always be improved. The translator can always learn more that would make it better, or can always think of a better way to write a sentence."[3]

Readers can therefore be confident that all differences that exist—between *Plaidoyer pour un renouveau de l'émotion en literature* and *The Seduction of Fiction*—have either been made by the author himself (he also made some small revisions to the original during the translation process), or have been approved by him as necessary to render the translation as readable as possible in English, while still giving "voice to the intention of the original."[4]

There now follows a list of changes, made always in aiming for harmony, as well as for clarity and grace; these changes are also exemplary of the conundrums and compromises besetting all translation endeavours, and perhaps of most interest and salience, in this case, to those who read both English and French and wish to compare the two versions.

The epigraph by Siri Hustvedt at the beginning of the book was chosen by the author and replaces one by Umberto Eco at the start of the French edition. It is a most apposite choice, for Hustvedt's passage seems to me to signpost most pertinently the central themes of this book, and enjoys the advantage of having been written for an English-speaking audience.

In the opening sentence of the Introduction, the author expresses sadness at a view expressed by Tzvetan Todorov. The original French is: "J'observe avec tristesse que de nos jours, 'lire des poèmes et des romans ne conduit pas à réfléchir sur la condition humaine, sur l'individu et la société, l'amour et la haine, la joie et le désespoir, mais sur *des notions critiques*, traditionnelles ou modernes.'" I translated this as: "It saddens me to agree with the observation that today 'to read poems and novels does not lead to reflection on the human condition, on the individual and society, on love and hate, joy and despair, but rather on *concepts of critique*, whether traditional or modern.'"

The French verb "observer" is used in the original in the sense of the English verb "to note." The author was noting sadly that Todorov's observation was still valid. But the English word "note" does not quite convey the depth of feeling inherent in the original sentence. My translation, therefore, "It saddens me to agree with the observation that today ...", although explicitly referencing Todorov's quotation, permits me to highlight both the author's agreement with the observation, and his sadness (by bringing that word to second place in the sentence), and seemed to me to convey more accurately the feeling of the original, a view with which the author agreed.

We encounter a different form of compromise on the last page of the Introduction, where I translated "la propriété fictive de la literature" for "the constructed nature of fiction." The explanation for this can be partially understood from the author's preface where he explains how the exigencies of formal French prose style in the original book compelled him to use the words "literature" and "fiction" "more or less synonymously." But it is obvious throughout the book that by "literature," Vernay means literary fiction. For this reason, I translated the French word "littérature" as "fiction" when I felt that word was more apposite, given its particular context, and as "literature" if a more general nuance was required. In the sentence in question, then, discussing readers who are knowledgeable in literary theories that focus on—and here I present a literal translation of the French—"the fictive property of literature," we end up with a phrase that sounds somewhat tautological in English. I therefore chose to translate it as "the constructed nature of fiction." For, as argued so eloquently in this book, fictional works are, above all, constructed worlds that seduce us into crossing their thresholds. In the same sentence, discussing our compassion for the adventures of fictional characters, the original French was "personnage romanesque." The word romanesque can connote highly imaginative or fantastic fables, but in this context, simply denotes fictional characters in a novel. But as the author has so far been discussing our emotional responses to reading literature (his previous sentence was about fictional space), my choice of English term was "fictional characters," with the adjective here denoting by default characters in novels.

A word is needed here about the pluralizing of this and some other terms throughout the English version which were formerly singular in the French. The fictional characters we have just been discussing, for example, were in fact singular in the original French. If I had kept to a single character, I would have been forced later in the sentence to use the masculine pronoun "he" as if it were generic, representing all characters, male and female, a practice that has been outdated for some time in English writing. In French, as many readers will know, a language with gendered nouns, the pronoun must correspond to the noun, not to any person's, or character's, actual gender. In English, the third person pronoun "they" is commonly used as a de facto gender-neutral singular pronoun in speech and in informal writing, but is not yet accepted as correct practice in academic discourse. For this reason, I pluralized nouns whenever it was necessary to avoid using a masculine pronoun as a so-called generic, so that "they" could be used as a legitimate gender-neutral pronoun. Throughout my translation, the nouns I pluralized most commonly were "readers" and "writers," in contexts where it would otherwise be impossible to provide a gender-neutral pronoun to refer to them. This particular conundrum and its compromise is an illuminating example of what lies between the source phrase and the target phrase, a space that has been termed "interliminal."[5]

The interliminal space can be most hazardous to navigate in contexts of deliberately chosen ambiguity, such as the following: The phrase "fabulation autorisée," which I have translated as "licensed fabrication," occurs four times in the book, first on the opening page of Chapter 6. The French word "fabulation" has several connotations: fantasizing, storytelling, lying, or telling a yarn or a tale. Although there is an English word "fabulation," with *a priori* similar connotations to the French word, it is not in common parlance, and in any case was appropriated some time ago by Robert Scholes to denote a specific type of fiction.

The best choice of English word to cover the range of ambiguity of the French word is "fabrication." It certainly covers deceptive utterances, which could include fantasizing, invention and faking, and since the author has taken great trouble arguing that storytelling is a mix of imagination and reality, this strengthens my choice of "fabrication" (for consistency's sake, I was then compelled to use "to fabricate" as the English verb for the French "fabuler," to tell stories, and "fabricated" as the adjective for "fabulé"). The only disadvantage of the English "fabrication" is that it carries a minor connotation of material production. Of equal challenge was the choice of accompanying adjective. The quite literal "authorized fabrication" is an unfamiliar collocation in English, except perhaps in manufacturing, and "licensed fabrication" shares this status. But the advantage of "licensed" over "authorized" is that it connotes entitlement and freedom, connotations most apposite in the context of storytelling. This particular interliminal navigation is an interesting example of how concepts will of necessity be mediated by the target language and culture.

This example also serves to highlight that any translation represents the limits of the translator's own reading, so this particular translation is necessarily my interpretation of what the work means to me at this time, an element in the boundary[6] that challenges all readers of writing that is not in their mother tongue. As translator, I was simultaneously the book's first reader in English, an exciting and privileged position that served to motivate me throughout the long process of making this book accessible to interested English readers worldwide.

University of Melbourne, Australia Carolyne Lee
March 2016

Notes

1. C. P. Snow, "The Rede Lecture, 1959," in C. P. Snow, *The Two Cultures: And a Second Look* (Cambridge: Cambridge University Press), 1959, 1964, 1–21.
2. Walter Benjamin, "The Task of the Translator," in *Illuminations*, ed. and intro. by Hannah Arendt, trans. Harry Zorn (London: Random House), 79.
3. Lydia Davis, "Some Notes on Translation and on Madame Bovary," *The Paris Review*, No. 198, Fall 2011, 88.
4. Benjamin, "Task of Translator", 79.
5. Marilyn Gaddis Rose, *Translation and Literary Criticism: Translation as Analysis* (Manchester, UK: St. Jerome Publishers), 1997, 7.
6. Ibid., 2.

Contents

Introduction

Abstract Vernay outlines his argument that contemporary teaching of literature rests on the arid concept of critique. Literary reflection has come to be dominated by a type of intellectual asphyxia, rather than a focus on the human condition. It would surely be better to show how the pleasure that literature provides can be useful, since emotional processes aid cognition, as advances in neurobiology have shown, leading to a rehabilitation of the "emotions." The Cartesian split between body and mind and its dissemination in the human sciences is vigorously argued against; and Vernay challenges us to permit the influence of emotion-charged fiction in order to open up the space of literary reflection, paving the way for a new psycholiterary approach.

Keywords Teaching of literature • Emotions • Cognition • Neurobiology • Psycholiterary approach

> … reading, as it had been taught to me in any event, gathered the strength of the idea and the excitement of the feelings, the generative beauty of the sentence and the subtle efficacy of the words, the constructed nature of the storytelling art, and the wrought complicity of the voice. It was all and is still interlinked, the meaning in the form, the form in the meaning.
>
> —Hubert Nyssen

It saddens me to agree with the observation that today "to read poems and novels does not lead to reflection on the human condition, on the individual and society, on love and hate, joy and despair, but rather on *concepts of critique*, whether traditional or modern."[1] This arid critical approach strips literature of affect and reduces it to verbal matter, provoking Tzvetan Todorov to declare, with some contrition, that "the contemporary method of teaching literature could hardly lead to a love of literature"[2]—a conclusion already reached by numerous higher education teachers on seeing the steady dwindling of enrollments in literature courses.[3] Perhaps we misguidedly followed the advice of Horace for whom poetry sought to be useful and to give pleasure (*prodesse et delectare*), when we should be endeavoring to prove how literature seeks to give pleasure in order to be useful. This could provide us with a pathway toward redressing the loss of interest in reading and literature that exists at all levels.

Indebted to advances in neurobiology, the rehabilitation of affect over the past three decades has, according to philosopher Michel Lacroix, given rise to "a new anthropology" which sees emotion "as an ally of reason, and which declares that in our deepest nature, we are *Homo sentiens* as much as *Homo sapiens*."[4] Indeed, contemporary society is swamped by a cult-like worship of the emotions, facilitating the exploitation by market forces of an inflated range of human arousal; we can add to this the neuroscientific arguments of Antoni Damasio for whom "… certain aspects of the process of emotion and feeling are indispensable for rationality."[5]

And yet not one theory of literature has incorporated these transformations.[6] It almost seems as if we believe readers are struck with alexithymia—the notorious pathological affliction whereby sufferers have difficulty expressing emotions. It is true that the old bipartite division of the brain into left hemisphere, the seat of reason and of logic, and right hemisphere, repository of the emotions and of intuition, did nothing to resolve the divorce between intellect and affects, so much so that emotions are almost always relegated to a level below the intellectual. But as we will see in this book, literature feeds on emotionalism, a fact to which the *Homo sentiens* reader would surely be responsive. Perhaps we should turn to a writer such as Christine Angot[7] where we find this disarmingly sincere if defiant declaration: "In literature, we lose a part of our heart as it goes to shape the book. It makes me cry because it's so emotionally draining. So I'm sobbing and crying, even if I'm happy at the same time."[8] Perhaps there is a chance that an equally exceptional "emotional person"[9] will be found among her readers, who will share many of her emotions on reading her novels. If this is the case, Michael Lacroix's plea for "a culture of emotional contemplation"[10] will not have been in vain.

This book is not just another meditation on literature and the status of fiction, nor on criticism and reading as socio-cultural and aesthetic practices; rather, it assumes the temper of a manifesto, with the audacious mission of taking a new look at literary tradition, while acknowledging the critical currents that have emerged during the twentieth century, and so far in the twenty-first century. The disconnect between emotion and judgment that has characterized many approaches to literary analysis derives ultimately from the division of body and mind that we find in Western philosophy (promoted especially by René Descartes), and aligned in the human sciences by an excessive valorization of the mind and pure reasoning, to the detriment of the body and the emotions. Because readers pay no heed to emotions, or repress them, they are oblivious to the pleasure the aesthetic enjoyment of a work can provide; while the dedicated teacher, who makes a point of structuring the learners' literary culture and who teaches technical interpretations of the text with great flair, can still fail to share the enjoyment of reading. In the wake of Jean-Paul Sartre's work on this subject, *Esquisse d'une théorie des émotions* (*Sketch for a Theory of the Emotions*, first published in Paris in 1939), a large body of scientific literature flourished in the 1980s–1990s, first delineating the emotions, and then analyzing their relationship with cognition.[11] The cognitive science approach reminds us of the mechanical nature of the human brain, and encourages us to recognize the contribution of the emotions to the intellectual process at the heart of the discipline of literature. This approach, too, raises new questions that I will discuss in the course of this book.

As a first step, we must make a distinction between the different communities of readers: a non-professional reader can be contrasted with a professional one, the main target audience of this work. This professional reader is skilled in literary interpretation, a competence that devotes itself to the art of treading a path between fidelity and liberty in confronting the uniqueness of the work in a wide-encompassing context that we cannot afford to overlook.

As for the writer, he or she is exposed as a professional seducer who struggles to win the readers' trust, via the narrator. We therefore have the right to ask how writers who sometimes denounce the artifice that makes the seduction possible can still manage to charm their readers. If this seduction is not the fruit of any literary trickery, is it conceived by the inherent alchemy of fiction? Do readers want or need to be seduced? To answer this, we have to turn to psychoanalysis which enjoys such symbiosis with literature that it could be expected to provide some answers. As licensed fabrication, fiction whets the appetite of readers for an imaginary world that often mimics or represents reality, without getting itself confused with reality. This is the reason why the fictional world is a space in which the notion of truth is problematic. For how can a reader knowledgeable in many literary theories on the constructed nature of fiction feel compassionate about the adventures of fictional characters, knowing perfectly well that they only exist on paper? It is logical to ask ourselves how something that does not exist can manage to generate real feelings in readers. For that matter, is the emotional involvement with literature the same for all readers, regardless of gender? Does the immersion in fiction facilitate the same identifications for all individuals, independently of their sexual identity and orientation, of their social class, and the "horizon of expectation"[12] in which the work is received? Finally, we come to the crucial question for everyone who experiences emotions: Who could claim to be impervious to emotional involvement in fiction when the very words are charged with affects?[13] This and so many other questions can serve to open up the space of literary reflection, deemed by some to be dominated by a type of intellectual asphyxia. It is in this context that psycholiterary analysis will, I hope, prove its worth.

Notes

1. T. Todorov, *La littérature en péril* (Paris: Flammarion, 2007), 18–19. Emphasis in the original.
2. Ibid., 25.
3. Michel Lacroix advances another argument: According to him, the trivialization of sexuality to increasingly younger audiences has desensitized the literary emotions of young people: "The prematurity of sexual life squanders one's propensity for sensitivity that could be available for aesthetic enjoyment. The leaps of imagination necessary for deriving delight from great works of fiction are thus foreclosed." *Le culte de l'émotion* (Paris: Flammarion, 2001), 141.
4. Ibid., 9.
5. A. Damasio, *Descartes' Error: Emotion, Reason and the Human Brain* (London & Basingstoke: Picador, 1994), xiii.
6. As can be inferred from his book, *André Breton* (Paris: José Corti, 1948), Julien Gracq's impressionistic criticism of him has a very affective dimension since he takes into account the impact of the literary work on the reader, but this does not exactly constitute a full and proper theory.

7. Translator's note: Christine Angot is a French writer whose confronting and often controversial work has explored the theme of incest, especially in her novels *L'inceste* and *Une semaine de vacances.*
8. C. Angot, *Une partie du coeur* (Paris : Stock, 2004), 86–87.
9. "The first characteristic of the emotional human being is to face fearlessly his emotions. They do not cause him to feel threatened, diminished or humiliated. Rather than repressing, he expresses, and even 'manages' them, as personal development experts would say." M. Lacroix, *Le culte de l'émotion*, 33.
10. Ibid., 147.
11. See P. Ekman, *Emotion in the Human Face* (Paris: Maison des Sciences de l'Homme, 1982); J. Maisonneuve, *Les sentiments*, coll. Que sais-je? (Paris: PUF, 1985); M. Pagès, *Trace ou sens. Le système émotionnel* (Paris: Hommes et groupes, 1986); J.-D. Vincent, *Biologie des passions* (Paris: Odile Jacob, 1986); A. Damasio, *Descartes' Error: Emotion, Reason and the Human Brain* (London & Basingstoke: Picador, 1994); J. LeDoux, *The Emotional Brain: The Mysterious Underpinnings of Emotional Life* (New York: Simon & Schuster, 1996); D. Goleman, *Emotional Intelligence: Why It Can Matter More Than IQ* (London: Bloomsbury, 1996), to cite only a few.
12. See Hans Robert Jauss, "Literary History as a Challenge to Literary Theory," trans. Elizabeth Benzinger, *New Literary History* 2.1 (1970), 7–37.
13. Even though the terms "affect" and "emotion" are often used synonymously, I would like to use psychological terminology to distinguish them: "One commonly accepted view is that affect is a broad and inclusive concept referring to both moods and emotions [...]. Moods in turn can be defined as relatively low-intensity, diffuse, and enduring affective states that have no salient antecedent cause and therefore little cognitive content (such as feeling good or feeling bad, being in a good or bad mood). In contrast, distinct emotions are more short-lived, intense phenomena and usually have a highly accessible and salient cause, as well as clear, prototypical cognitive content (e.g., disgust, anger, or fear). Both emotions and moods may have an impact on social cognition, but the nature of this influence is quite different." In J.P. Forgas, Introduction to J.P. Forgas (ed.), *Feeling and Thinking: The Role of Affect in Social Cognition* (Cambridge: CUP/Maison des Sciences de l'Homme, 2001), 6.

CHAPTER 1

The Multiple Possibilities of Reading

Abstract Two types of reader are delineated: the non-professional and the professional (literary critics, teachers, etc.). Directing his argument to the latter, Vernay surveys the critical theories that dominated the twentieth century, arguing that they all prioritized "scientific principles," objectifying interpretation, discouraging readers from expressing feelings. Compelled to write "scientific reports" of books, students have turned away from reading. We should aim instead for "active appropriation," based on the alchemy of intellect and emotions, whereby readers as co-creators of texts aim not so much to discover what texts mean, as how they achieve results. Feelings will make literature intelligible; it is thus the "impression" a reader forms that is important, here offered as an approach for reading a text, a way of attracting new generations of readers.

Keywords Professional reader • Non-Professional reader • Literary critics • Active appropriation • Intellect • Emotions • Readers' impressions

> At the level of discursive structure the reader is invited to fill up various empty phrastic spaces (texts are lazy machineries that ask someone to do part of their job). At the level of narrative structures, the reader is supposed to make forecasts concerning the future course of the fabula. … Every text … is in some way making the addressee expect (and foresee) the fulfilment of every unaccompanied sentence …
>
> —Umberto Eco

© The Editor(s) (if applicable) and The Author(s) 2016
J.-F. Vernay, *The Seduction of Fiction*,
DOI 10.1007/978-3-319-39453-4_1

Let us shout it from the rooftops: Literature provides a space so rich with possibilities because it is able to offer much more than expression or revelation. The text, like illusion and representation, is but a mere façade concealing a subtext that begs to be discovered. The explicit part is only the tip of the iceberg, as the unfathomable unspoken element brims with messages brought to the surface by the reader's interpretation. On the whole, there are two ways of reading: "one, naïve and innocent, 'in the first degree', as we sometimes say; the other fierce and critical." It would therefore be convenient to leave it at "this tension between the state of rapture and the delights of critical attention [which] is the very lifeblood of reading."[1]

There are, in general, two types of readers: the professional reader, and the non-professional reader. I intend to categorize as "professional reader" (Umberto Eco speaks of the "Model Reader," the one who "wants to know how the story has been told"[2]) anyone ***under an obligation to read***, whether in an institutional or professional context. This may include journalists, booksellers, librarians, literary critics, editors, proofreaders, teachers, or students required to study a work. Professional readers fulfill their duty because it is required. For them, reading does not constitute diversion (as understood by French philosopher Pascal) and may well be demanding. It should be noted that the reading habits of professional readers present constraints, although there are some compensations. These people are not always permitted to choose their reading, for example, which exempts them from the influence of socio-economic factors; reading is not in competition with other forms of entertainment (such as films, games, and sport). Another constraint is that professional readers have no choice but to make themselves available for this exercise but, seen from another angle, since this reading does not have to compete with their other pursuits, it will never be put off on the grounds that these readers cannot find the time to read. The professional reader, even if forced to read at a more demanding level, retains some flexibility in unraveling the text, such as questioning the text further in order to explore the range of effects. In this space of freedom, the reader

> … decides whether the text has two or more levels of meaning, whether it's worth looking for an allegorical sense, or whether the tale is also saying something about the reader—and whether these different senses blend together in a solid and harmonious form, or whether they can float about independent of one another.[3]

Meanwhile, non-professional readers (whom Eco would qualify as "semantic" in *On Literature*, as those who only "want to know what happens")[4] are influenced by socio-economic factors (i.e., they can choose to see the film adaptation of a literary work rather than read it), and by the time that they wish to devote to reading. Those who read on public transport, for example, might prefer shorter narratives. And if recreation is the goal, such as reading on the beach, lighter content will be favored. Even if confining oneself to a semantic reading, the non-professional reader—cousin of Eco's "empirical reader"—has complete latitude in approaching the text: "Empirical readers can read in many ways, and there is no law that tells them how to read, because they often use the text as a container for their own passions, which may come from outside the text, or which the text may arouse by chance."[5] While presenting a sociology of reading is outside my current aims, it can be shown precisely at what point certain observations must be qualified, such as those by Daniel Pennac in his book *Reads Like a Novel*. Pennac believes that "Man … reads because he knows he's alone. His reading keeps him company, but without replacing any other; rather, no other company can take its place."[6] Beyond this metaphysical dimension that would only apply to the non-professional reader, there are many other ways to justify "this act of permanent creation."[7]

I will focus here on the professional reader only. In his preface to the French edition of Hans Robert Jauss' book, *Pour une esthétique de la réception* (published in English as *Towards an Aesthetic of Reception*), Starobinski unintentionally gives a perfect definition of the literary critic, who can be seen as the most accomplished of readers:

> The reader is therefore at once, or by turns, the one who occupies the role of receiver, of discriminator (in the sense of the basic critical function of accepting or rejecting), and in some cases the producer, imitating or, arguably, reinterpreting an existing work.[8]

We can essentially map professional reading by distinguishing three ways of "creating." A bird's eye view will confirm that one can take an interest by turns in, first, the text (writing-oriented); second, the author (writer oriented); and third, the reader (reader-oriented). The fact that many literary theories have privileged one exclusive approach is regrettable for several reasons, but we do need to recognize that their legacy is invaluable.

Among the theories that developed around the text in the first half of the twentieth century, in Europe, there was Genetic Criticism[9] which focused its attention on the pretext (namely, the historicity of the literary material); socio-criticism, which gives the text a socialization value, in establishing a strong relationship between society and the literary work; and then, the formalist method with its fervent proponents such as Victor Schklovsky and Roman Jakobsen. Strongly inspired by linguistics, the Russian formalists devoted themselves to rendering intelligible the literary material by examining its "literariness,"[10] and by emphasizing its "internal laws" that governed the development of the work. Later, in the 1950s, genre theory, eminently represented by Northrop Frye,[11] stylistics, poetics, semiotics, narratology, and New Criticism (and structuralism, deconstruction, and post-structuralism) concerned themselves only with the actual text, usually considered as an autonomous, closed space. In the early 1980s, Jean Bellemin-Noël conceived his groundbreaking textual analysis, granting each text its own unconscious, no hypallage intended!

Then along came the currents of literary criticism that swirled around the figure of the author: The critique of consciousness (with adherents such as Jean Rousset and Jean Starobinski), focusing on the writing subject, while psychocriticism had as its raison d'être the exploration of the author's unconscious.

And finally, in answer to New Criticism, reader-response theory reserved the best role for readers, out of faith in their capacity to transform the text. This theory, attributed in Anglophone scholarship to Stanley Fish and Wolfgang Iser, is midway between "non-Marxist sociology of literature"[12] and poetics. It fell mainly to Wolfgang Iser and Hans Robert Jauss, from the "Constance School"[13] to develop an aesthetic of reception (*Rezeption-Aesthetik*), especially from 1967, when Jauss outlined the basic principles. These principles established "a distinction between the effect (*Wirkung*), determined by the work, maintaining links with the past in which the work originated, and with its reception which depends on the free, active recipient, judging according to the aesthetic norms of the time, modifying the terms of the dialogue by his own existence …"[14]

Clearly, all these methods of critical analysis, involving a desire to establish a literary science, did not encourage the staging of a confrontation of different approaches. But to have a wider perspective, it would have been absolutely necessary to be equally interested in the three modes of perceiving writing: taking into account the past (focusing on the author, the source of the text), the present (discovering the text in question), and the future (highlighting the text's potential, which will in time be revealed by a multiplicity of readings).

We must now turn to focus on the reader who brings the text to life by creating meaning. We can safely say that a literary text is a linguistic construct resulting from a mental structure that resists, represents, or enriches reality. Unlike a treasure awaiting discovery by an explorer, the text expects no revelation from the reader. Neither does the author endeavor to encode his text, as Dan Brown does, for example, so that the meaning will only be perceptive to the cleverest readers. If this were the case, all literature would be cryptofiction, a far cry from what I am arguing. I prefer to think of *the literary text as a mental construct, freighted with affect and loaded with meaning that will gradually surface, invoked by the respective sensitivities of each reader who interacts with it emotionally*. The reader's role is therefore to try and understand not so much what the text means, as how it achieves its results. It is accordingly feelings (through cognitive processes which solicit perception by means of sense organs) that will make the literary text intelligible, even if reading is defined as an intellectual and physiological activity that passes in transit from the eyes to the brain.

Understanding how the literary text operates does not mean reconstructing its main elements with factual accuracy. Generations of teachers demanded of their students this limiting performance, an exercise that was mainly a response to a fantasy—that of seeing literary analysis elevated to a science. Formerly, as Tzvetan Todorov pointed out, literary history was confined either to "a study of the causes that lead to the publication of the work: social forces, political, ethnic, psychological, of which the literary text was supposed to be the result;" or else to an analysis of the "effects of this text, its distribution, its impact on the public, and its influence on other writers. The insertion of the literary work into a causal chain was thus given preference."[15] These were the beginnings of a scientific process that saw a text as causing certain effects to be analyzed, or inversely as an effect for which one had to find the cause. Parallel to these investigations, for decades literary theorists tried to outperform scientists with their Cartesian way of approaching literature through theorizing schemas (the hobby horse of Russian Formalists such as Vladimir Propp and Tzvetan Todorov), through the release of conceptual structures (see, for example, narratology, invented by structuralism, led by figures such as Roland Barthes, A. J. Greimas, and Gérard Genette), and prioritizing analytical approaches based to a certain extent on scientific principles. Exactly what these theorists sought to do was neither more nor less than to objectify interpretation.

We still see the direct consequence of this movement in our schools today, for example, with the majority of secondary students. We are still training young minds to make a detailed summary of a story, to find the signposts, to know the most minute detail, however insignificant: an exercise in literary dissection which does not encourage readers to express their feelings, nor to develop a critical outlook by promoting a wider perspective on the story and its concerns. Pierre Bayard notes that this "catastrophic exercise," which is akin to "a kind of scientific record, does not correlate with how readers read, and may well turn them away from reading."[16] According to Bayard, "to read does not mean to mechanically record, but to create."[17] Such an approach would allow readers to express their feelings rather than confining them to passive responses.

Admittedly, there are readers who have a "need to interpret," and for whom the literary text tends to exist "literally and in every way," in the words of Rimbaud.[18] But it seems that creators of texts deploy abundant ingenuity to put readers off the track and make their task more difficult; as Octave Mannoni said so aptly in *Clefs pour l'imaginaire ou l'autre scène,* poetic art "is not the art of indulging in the metaphor game and discovering that anything can be said about anything, but is the art of concealment, of providing sufficient justification, to orient the reader to something else …"[19] It is worth repeating: The text does not expect any revelation from the reader, but literature lays bare an enigma or, to quote Roland Barthes, asks "an indirect question" to which each reader brings his or her personal response.

> To write is to jeopardize the meaning of the world, to put an *indirect* question that the writer, by an ultimate abstention, refrains from answering. It is each of us who gives the answer, bringing to it his own history, his own language, his own freedom; but since history, language, and freedom are infinitely variable, the world's answer to the writer is infinite: there is no end to answering what has been written beyond hope of an answer: asserted, disputed, superseded—the meanings pass, the question remains.[20]

Literary creation would seem, then, to create a gap of uncertainty, ranging from narrow to wide, a gap that a close reading tends to reduce in the act of recreation. Not only is it the task of professional readers to unravel a web of linguistic signs in order to explore the range of possible interpretations, but they must also give the text a second life by restoring the understanding that they have, attuned to their sensitivity. It is this alchemy of the intellectual and the emotional that is responsible for the "realisation of literary texts on the part of the receptive reader," as Hans Robert Jauss reminds us in *Toward an Aesthetic of Reception*.[21] In short, "only the act of reading assumes the 'realisation' of literary works."[22] Jauss rightly sees "the reception of works [as] an active ownership, which modifies the value and meaning through the generations."[23] Active appropriation happens as much from the sensitivity of readers, resonant with their experience, as from the critical judgment that develops what I call, if I may venture this Genette-style neologism, a hyperconstruction. Logically, the literary text in this binary relation will be a hypoconstruction.[24]

In this professional reader-centered hermeneutic process, what is important is not so much the factual rendition of the work, but the impression readers form after reading the story. In other words, the reader takes a look at the text and passes that impression on to other readers in order to illuminate the work's complexity and "pluri-dimensionality."[25] Any analysis made should not be prescriptive but rather offer suggestions, in the sense that it offers a point of view for a reading of the text. The discerning critic will favor the pertinence of the point of view which will provide an enlightened or original reading, whether generic or specific.

It appears, in fact, that literary analysis comes down to the writer's sensitivity intersecting with the reader's. It is in my view this affective dimension, repressed for years by the New Criticism, which would benefit from a resurgence in literary studies to attract a new generation of young students. I will return to this point in my final chapter, but before that I wish to pursue my examination of the role of the professional reader who, after having read (or should I say "skim-read")[26] the works, must be a critic (and not a writer!)[27] in order to give his impressions and opinions.

Notes

1. M. Raimond, *Le roman* (Paris: Armand Colin/HER, 2000 [1987]), 5–6.
2. U. Eco, *On Literature*, translated by Martin McLaughlin (NY: Harcourt, 2000), 220–223.
3. Ibid., 223.
4. Ibid., 223.
5. U. Eco, *Six Walks in the Fictional Woods* (Cambridge, Mass.: Harvard University Press), 8.
6. D. Pennac, *Reads Like a Novel* (London: Quartet Books, translated by Daniel Gunn, 1994), 177.

7. Ibid., 27.
8. J. Starobinski, Preface to H.R. Jauss, *Pour une esthétique de la réception* (Paris: Gallimard, 1978), 13.
9. A European alternative to Anglo-American criticism, this has best been described in the following way in *Genetic Criticism*, edited by Jed Deppman, Daniel Ferrer, and Michael Groden: "… the chief concern [of genetic criticism] is not the 'final' text but the reconstruction and analysis of the writing process. Geneticists find endless richness in what they call the 'avant-texte': a critical gathering of a writer's notes, sketches, drafts, manuscripts, typescripts, proofs, and correspondence." (Philadelphia: University of Pennsylvania Press, 2004). See: http://www.textualscholarship.org/gencrit/index.html.
10. A concept proposed by Roman Jakobson in 1921.
11. It should be noted that the French critic Jean-Yves Tadié classed Frye in the category of "criticism of the imaginary", as well as Gaston Bachelard, Jean-Pierre Richard, and Gilbert Durand, the last-named famous for *Les structures anthropologiques de l'imaginaire* (1960). J.-Y. Tadié, *La critique littéraire au XX* e *siècle* (Paris: Belfond, 1987), 107–130.
12. J.-Y. Tadié, *La critique littéraire*, 183.
13. This was a movement founded at the University of Constance by Jauss and colleagues, based on eighteenth century German philosophy, focussing on the interaction between subjects and objects.
14. J. Starobinski in H.R. Jauss, *Pour une esthétique*, 19.
15. T. Todorov, *La littérature en péril*, 30.
16. P. Bayard and U. Eco, "Ce que lire veut dire", *Le Magazine littéraire* 487 (June 2009), 14.
17. Ibid., 15.
18. A. Rimbaud cited in O. Mannoni, *Clefs pour l'imaginaire ou l'autre scène* (Paris: Le Seuil, 1969), 202.
19. Ibid., 216.
20. R. Barthes, Foreword in *On Racine*, trans. Richard Howard (Berkeley and Los Angeles: University of California Press, 1992), ix.
21. H.R. Jauss, *Toward an Aesthetic of Reception*, translated by Timothy Bahti, Introduction by Paul de Man (Minneapolis: University of Minnesota Press, 1982). "History of literature is a process of aesthetic reception and production that takes place in the realization of literary texts on the part of the receptive reader, the reflective critic, and the author in his continuing productivity." 21.
22. Ibid., 13.
23. Ibid., 17.
24. The terminology hyperconstruction/hypoconstruction is a homage to Genette's hypertext/hypotext. Hyperconstruction is the critic's interpretation of a text which results in a new construct. Hypoconstruction is the text

which is being interpreted and which is the writer's construct that comes first in this binary writer/critic relationship.

25. J. Derrida, *Of Grammatology*, translated by Gayatri Chakravorty Spivak (Baltimore: Johns Hopkins Press, 1978), 85.
26. Pierre Bayard is fond of using this verb (skim-read) in his *How to Talk About Books You Haven't Read*, to show us how the act of reading can be undermined by anxieties about fairness (not to favor one reading over another, so ending up reading nothing), the need to give an overview (so stick to summaries and blanket descriptions), the spread of ideas (mixing personal with others' experiences which only confuses), not to mention memory failure, all cautioning us to be more careful in using the verb "read!"
27. For Fabrice Thumerel, the writer and the critic "certainly use the evocative force of figures ... this force does not have the same value across both activities: the writer favours the *locutionary* act and criticizes the illocutionary act—in other words, the first one seeks, in the most original way possible, *to create meaning*, while the second aims to change the direction, the knowledge, and to influence the reader in orienting him towards a particular interpretation of the text". F. Thumerel, *La critique littéraire* (Paris: Armand Colin, 2002), 37.

CHAPTER 2

Interpretation as an Art

Abstract An active form of literary criticism, "hyperconstruction"' is a neologism that encompasses a plurality of interpretations, without meaning there will be no limits to interpretation. Following Eco, we must respect the text's intention, but line-by-line analyses and essays for formal examinations militate against a love of books. Similarly, contemporary book reviews "interrogate" the text rather than showing a love of literature, rendering the book an "object." Vernay instead offers a type of book review to add value to a literary work, rather than drowning it in metadiscourse. A critic should transmit a love of reading, but instead literature has been dehumanized and desensitized. To counter this, critics could write in the first person, to express their feelings, conveying the "pleasure of the text."

Keywords Literary criticism • Hyperconstruction • Umberto Eco • Pleasure of the text

> … every criticism is a criticism of the work *and* a criticism of itself.
>
> —Roland Barthes

My own experience in literary criticism, or my hyperconstructing experience—a terminology in keeping with the discussion thus far—has shown me to what extent interpreting a text has attained the status of an art form. So I have often wondered how to talk about books you *have*

© The Editor(s) (if applicable) and The Author(s) 2016

J.-F. Vernay, *The Seduction of Fiction*,
DOI 10.1007/978-3-319-39453-4_2

read. This Bayard-pastiching question refers to the concept of "the open work," dear to Umberto Eco, encouraging a plurality of interpretations. To recapitulate Eco's analysis,

> … the form of the work of art gains its aesthetic validity precisely in proportion to the number of different perspectives from which it can be viewed and understood. These give it a wealth of different resonances and echoes without impairing its original essence …[1]

A plurality of interpretations is justified by the "horizon of expectations" (Jauss's terminology, influenced by Husserl's phenomenology) peculiar to each reader. But all reading has potential pitfalls, against which we should guard. Eco, good semiotician that he is, does not waste the opportunity to warn us about a deconstructionist position, according to which one can do whatever one wants with a book,[2] something one risks if following this line to the letter. In his chapter "On some functions of literature," Eco reminds readers of their dual obligation:

> Reading works of literature forces on us an exercise of fidelity and respect, albeit within a certain freedom of interpretation. There is a dangerous critical heresy, typical of our time, according to which we can do anything we like with a work of literature, reading into it whatever our most uncontrolled impulses dictate to us. This is not true.[3]

We are now beset with a double bind: How to carry out, with factual precision, an inadvisable "exercise in fidelity" without due deference to the literary text or overdoing factual precision? How to give rein to our free interpretation without easily making the mistake of doing "anything we like with a text?" For Eco, the response is simple. The practice of fidelity is about respecting "the intention of the text," which sets limits to interpretation:

> Literary works encourage freedom of interpretation, because they offer us a discourse that has many layers of reading and place before us the ambiguities of language and of real life. But in order to play this game, which allows every generation to read literary works in a different way, we must be moved by a profound respect for what I have called elsewhere the intention of the text.[4]

Without limits to interpretation, the boundary between *speaking of* a literary work and *speaking about* a work will become so porous that it would be difficult to make the distinction between the mock reader and the actual reader. Those who do not read yet decide to speak about the book to hide their ignorance

> "will excel at the inflationary art of commentary (I read ten lines, I produce ten pages), at the head-shrinker's practice of writing reports (I flick through 400 pages, I reduce them to five), and at fishing for judicious quotations (in those deep-frozen cultural 'digests' which are available in all success-stores). They'll succeed in manipulating the scalpel of line by line analysis, and will become experts in skillful navigating among 'selected extracts', all of which will doubtless lead to success in the baccalaureate, a university degree, and even to success in the advanced, national competitive test, the *agrégation*. But all of which will not necessarily lead to a love for books."[5]

Is it not the job of the well-informed and creative reader to produce a commentary which is by definition inflated in comparison with the literary text? To simplify it at first and then to give an account of its complexities? To underline the purple passages (effects of style, original thoughts, reflective sections, etc.), thus paying tribute to the writer's work? At first glance, it is not so easy to differentiate the mock reader from the real reader. That said, it is extremely difficult for the mock reader to continue deceiving beyond a few lines.

But of what use is a review? The book review today takes it upon itself to interrogate the text: an activity which does not lead to the transmission of a relish for reading, nor to sharing the love of literature. There is even precious little discussion about the sensuality of the book as object—the allure of the cover, the touch and smell of the pages, the whisper of the words—pleasures that electronic reading devices will soon obscure if not entirely oust.

For Jean-Paul Sartre, "reading is induction, interpolation, extrapolation"[6]: Induction because one must infer certain things in order to extrapolate, and it is here that we come to the idea that reading is an act of creation. The phenomenon of interpolation can be accounted for by the fact that criticism slides insidiously into the cracks of the literary edifice, producing a critical summary larded with quotations from the work. This type of reviewing is a particular literary exercise in the course of which literature ceases to be the aesthetic and intellectual message of a writer and becomes an object … of study.

With his characteristic wit, Pierre Bayard manages to find a use for the book review, suggesting that it is an element in this vast ensemble that he calls the "collective library" which according to him, "we do not need to know comprehensively in order to appreciate any one of its elements … The trick is to define the book's place in that library, which gives it meaning in the same way a word takes on meaning in relation to other words."[7] Determining the position of the book will only happen through the perspective of the professional reader whose positioning is infused with his own ideology and ethics.

In my mainly subjective explanatory critical practice (of which the motto would be: know, describe, and explain), the choice of book and author are paramount because it is not so much about providing a reading formula as about sharing one's sensibility as a reader in order to illuminate a work's multiple levels of meaning. Far be it from me to imply here that texts I select be of a certain opacity, or even less be totally opaque! If it were not for their ability to present a dense structure in order to reveal several layers of meaning, these novels would be uninteresting and tedious to me.

In my view, criticism could be conceived as an added value to a literary work. Consequently, it must contain neither wordiness (against which Roland Barthes warns us in his *Criticism and Truth*), nor paraphrase—a shortcoming I encounter often in student essays, more rarely in scholarly articles. For any literature lover, the exercise of an objective review would surely be felt as an annihilation of one's subjectivity, given that criticism tends to dilute literature in a flood of metadiscourse which ends up standing in for the literary work itself. It is a sad moment for all teachers when they realize their students prefer to read the study notes on a set text instead of the real thing. This is the reason I spoke of hypo- and hyperconstructions in the previous chapter, since hyperconstruction (or critical material) always ends up eclipsing hypoconstruction (the literary work).

But what exactly is a critic? The "essential characteristics of the critic," that Guy de Maupassant pointed out in 1887, are still salient today: "He must be without bias, without opinions or preconceived ideas, without links to institutions or ties to schools of thought, but must understand, distinguish and explain the most contrasting trends, the most contrary temperaments, and recognize the most diverse works of art."[8] In being critical, the professional reader stops reading for entertainment and actively seeks to understand the work in order to give a rendition of it. When I read a work, I do not seek to determine its intrinsic qualities since they are all relative and vary according to the era and the readership. What I am trying to do above all is to transmit the love of reading the authors on which I comment. In order to do this, it is in my view necessary to break with the tradition of a metadiscourse that is stultifying for at least two reasons: It is awash with pedantic literary jargon (even though sometimes offset by a glossary at the end of the book); and it monotonously fixates on form. This is what is behind literature's dehumanization and desensitization.

The desensitization in French formal literary criticism comes from the love of using impersonal turns of phrase (such as "it is necessary to examine ..."), or the royal "we" which paradoxically denotes a participatory rhetoric as much as it constructs a condescending distance between professional and non-professional readers. Trained in this tradition myself, I am as guilty as anyone! But why not be inspired by the impressionist criticism of Julien Gracq and occasionally make use of the first person singular to express the reasons why we like or do not like a novel? We must, however, guard against falling into "preferential discourse," in the sense in which Bernard Vouilloux[9] uses the term, and indulging bouts of egotism. Although impressionist criticism can be very worthwhile, because it gives sway to the reader's emotions and impressions, it tends to foster fragmentary discourse, whereas I am seeking to give the whole picture, other than that originally given by the novel. That said, if we observe an impressionist painting with its small brushstrokes that the artist has striven to juxtapose, we can perceive a coherent unity. It is not fragmentation that emanates from such art, but instead a harmonious ensemble.

To foster a love of reading is also to communicate "the pleasure of the text"—an advantage that must surely see literature get even with the sciences!—or even to acknowledge the text's "jouissance," or pleasure (Roland Barthes), a feature that helps counter the trivialization of literature and its reduction to a mere cultural object to be consumed.[10] I am inclined to believe that the seductive pleasure is not solely derived from the dual aesthetics of the text—namely the visual aesthetic related to the descriptive imagery, and the auditory aesthetic that we perceive through the melody of the words. No wonder Flaubert went through what he termed the "reading-aloud test" (*l'épreuve du gueuloir*). Seduction also operates on a mental level. It is, therefore, important to enhance the underlying connections to the text that stimulate a reader's capacity to draw parallels, and to glimpse the networks of ideas suggested by the text.

If the writer is subject to a set of diverse influences (on which I will elaborate in the next chapter), so too is the critic. I would also willingly align myself with David Birch's opinion that "the way you construct meanings for texts depends on the way you construct theories about the world—about realities."[11] It is surely self-evident that all professional readers who are bound by a methodology are necessarily nurtured by ideologies that influence their discourse and disclose their convictions which, in turn, seep through the words on the page.

Notes

1. U. Eco, *The Open Work*, translated by Anna Cancogni (Cambridge, Mass.: Harvard University Press, 1989), 3.
2. U. Eco, *On Literature*, translated by Martin McLaughlin (Orlando, Florida: Harcourt, 2004), 4.
3. Ibid.
4. Ibid.
5. D. Pennac, *Reads Like a Novel*, translated by Daniel Gunn (London: Quartet Books, 1994), 91–92.
6. J.-P. Sartre, *What is Literature?* translated by Bernard Frechtman (London & NY: Routledge, 1950/2001), 40.
7. P. Bayard, *How to Talk About Books You Haven't Read*, translated by Jeffrey Mehlman (London: Bloomsbury, 2007), 117.
8. G. de Maupassant, "Le roman", Préface de *Pierre et Jean* (Paris: Pocket, 2006), 13.
9. B. Vouilloux cited in F. Thumerel, *La critique littéraire*, 125.
10. Ibid., 15.
11. D. Birch, *Language, Literature and Critical Practice* (London/New York: Routledge, 1989), 25.

CHAPTER 3

Context Matters

Abstract Acknowledging the influence of New Criticism on literary studies, Vernay notes that conceptualizing a literary text as an enclosed space does not take into account the different forces that have participated in the creation of the work. The influence of these forces on the text is often ignored, something that could be related to anxieties about imitation. But influence is not confined only to literary aspects. The text is also at the mercy of hidden editorial forces which go as far as impacting on the style, tone, and format of the book as object.

Keywords New Criticism • Literary studies • Imitation • Editorial

> Literature is not conceived in a vacuum, but in a crucible of living speech with which it shares many features …
>
> —Tzvetan Todorov

The novel—whether it be "engaged" or "disengaged," to quote Georges Perec[1]—emerges as a multifaceted genre due to its remarkable capacity to renew itself on so many levels: thematic, aesthetic, even deontological. If the text has enough resources to be the subject of a good analysis, it will give its full measure only after having been illuminated in its context, in which the publishing world plays a part.

Adherents of New Criticism, who see the literary work as a hermetic and self-sufficient linguistic system, would almost have us believe that

© The Editor(s) (if applicable) and The Author(s) 2016

J.-F. Vernay, *The Seduction of Fiction*,
DOI 10.1007/978-3-319-39453-4_3

"the work imposes the advent of an order that ruptures the existing state of affairs, the affirmation of a rule that obeys its own logic and law."[2] There is something quite peculiar about this need to see the text as an enclosed space in order that it be open to a plurality of interpretations, but that is indeed the underlying intention of New Criticism not wishing to be burdened with the author's views. It was then very convenient to divest authors of all authority over their texts by proclaiming their symbolic death (as did Roland Barthes), to deny the autobiographical dimension of a text by rejecting out of hand any link between the life of the author and his work, and simply overlooking the part played by social forces in novels.[3] It remains to be seen whether such a categorical stance could be improved by being more nuanced.

Textual self-sufficiency—a Modernist principle taken over by New Criticism—gives primacy to the word over the world. To declare a text free from any influence is the best means of ridding critics of all interpretive inhibitions. As a result, "it is unsurprising that pupils learn the dogmatic view that literature is unrelated to the rest of the world, and study only the internal relations between the elements of the work."[4] Based on this premise, anything and everything becomes acceptable: By not taking into account contextual factors, criticism will not privilege one particular reading over any other. But it would be difficult to identify theoretical contributions, underlying cultural elements, and any traces of intertextuality—whether borrowings, influences, or simple allusions—without information on the following contexts: genetic, in order to trace literary descent; historical, especially for historical or political novels; and biographical, surely unavoidable for novels that have been termed "roman du moi."[5]

A vision of the literary text that is deprived of such richness may well be incomplete, if not naïve, and even more so if the information is available! Of course, this problem does not arise for anonymous works, nor for those by ancient authors. As Pierre Bayard so aptly said, "For many ancient authors, it is hardly contestable that our complete ignorance of their personalities, of their circumstances, or of their lives or creations is no disadvantage in appreciating their work and making an informed judgment about them."[6]

Why did New Criticism wish to hide the power of influence—whether of one text on another, or of a context on a text? Could it be linked to the unease that influence generates, an unease identified in Freudian terms by Harold Bloom in his seminal work, *The Anxiety of Influence: A Theory of*

Poetry (1973). Influence is a phenomenon that few authors will readily admit due to the thin and porous border between influence and imitation. While influence is seen as the ability to "fecundate," as T. S. Eliot pertinently observed, imitation "can only sterilize." [7] That being the case, the writer would pass for an imitator who would write "in the manner of" right up to being accused of plagiarism. No doubt many discerning readers will view imitation as an admission of impotence, or even worse: a dried-up imagination! But this fear has not been borne out, as evidenced by the absurd and very funny 2009 book by Pierre Bayard, *Le plagiat par anticipation* (Anticipated plagiarism), a work that chronologically reverses issues of influence.

Each text is written in a context that should not be ignored, for why else would authors leave paratextual clues in their work? It is done in response to two basic needs: the popularization and readability of their plots. Indeed, it is likely that writers do this to expand their readership beyond Umberto Eco's Model Readers (on whom nothing is lost because they possess encyclopedic knowledge, required for a detailed reading) and to provide keys for comprehending the complexity of the work.

The question of context is essential for any "literature in the second degree" (Gérard Genette), particularly in the case of pastiches, parodies, and text-palimpsests. For those, it would be wise to adapt the reasoning behind the translation principle (based on the dialectic of the original and the copy) to the mechanisms of the hypotext and hypertext, to reprise Genette's terminology. In fact, one can see that the difference that emerges after rewriting is inherent in the original (read: hypotext). To return to George Steiner's idea, rewriting (be it a translation or the hypertext pastiche) provides the original with a "spatial and temporal resonance" and serves as a telling measure for it, a process that makes the transformations visible in a new textual space (read: hypertext):

> Supreme translation ... makes live restitution to the original not only in that it gives to it a new range of spatial and temporal resonance, not only in that it can illuminate the original, compelling it, as it were, into greater clarity and impact. The process of reciprocation goes much deeper. A great translation bestows on the original *that which was already there*. It augments the original by externalizing, by deploying visibly, elements of connotation, of overtone and undertone, latencies of significance, affinities with other texts and cultures or defining contrasts with these—all of which are present, are "there" in the original from the outset but may not have been fully declared.[8]

In other words, variation emerges through the phenomenon of transposition, thanks to another context, but for all that it is not the result of any contribution from without—the difference being contained within the body of the original: Against all expectations, the hypertext can achieve no originality without the original. What is valid for the creative process applies to interpreting: Any close reading of a text that aims at originality cannot dispense with the original (that is, the hypotext, or context).

If one wishes to know what types of influence affect the aesthetic work, and how they are going to change our perception of the literary text, it would be unwise not to take into account the publishing world. To take an interest in the work as publication is to note the passage of the manuscript from the private sphere of the author to the public exposure of it through marketing. In other words, it means factoring in the economic logic in which the work is inscribed, without necessarily making the literary text a pretext for a Marxist analysis of the laws of production and profit inherent in the book market. Since this is about literature and not economics, the aesthetic work must remain our central concern.

When culture started to become mass produced, from around the end of the 1970s, Marthe Robert directed our attention to the desecration of literature and to the birth of what I will call "the marketing-modified book," a book reduced to nothing more than a commercial commodity tailored to popular tastes.

> No longer something crucial and compelling, literature has no more prestige or interest than any other cultural product, and indeed is forced to provide some justification for its privileged status. It can no longer rest on its laurels and must henceforth consent to become one of many controlled objects, or admit that it is an outdated myth.[9]

Unlike publishers who are all too aware of this fact, consumers, referred to out of aesthetic prudishness as "readers," often forget that a published text immediately becomes a "book object," and what seems to be part of a "literary production" remains nonetheless a "marketing product," involving a number of actors in the production cycle. For Alain Finkielkraut, "it was the instrumental reason or 'calculative thinking', to use Heidegger's phrase, that relegated meditative thinking (what we are calling culture) to the realm of entertainment."[10] And the philosopher concluded his book *The Defeat of the Mind* (1987) by sounding the swan song:

> So barbarism has finally colonized culture. In the shadow of this great word, intolerance grows at the same pace as infantilism. When it is not cultural identity boxing up individuals in their groups and which, under penalty of high treason, refuses all access to doubt, irony, and reason—all that would disconnect the individual from the collective mould, it is the leisure industry, this creation of the technical age, which reduces intellectual works to dross (or, as they say in America, to "entertainment").[11]

These days, the publishing industry—claiming to be responding to consumer demand—has changed so much in the way that it presents the novel. To guarantee authors a loyal readership, publishers have three requirements: simplicity, readability, and reliability. How can we comment either positively or negatively on the stylistics or aesthetics of a work if "the entertainment industry" reduces it to dross, as Finkielkraut said above? It is precisely on this point that a pluralistic perspective could make a difference to the critical appraisal of literary works.

No doubt professional readers will be called upon to make a distinction between two types of publishing: independent or niche market publishers which allow their authors the discretion of developing their chosen structure and style, while remaining confined to a limited readership; and general publishers who are more interested in the profitability of their publication than in the possibility of welcoming a potential or actual Nobel Prize-winning writer into their stable.

Notes

1. In "Powers and limits of the contemporary French novelist", a conference held at the University of Warwick May 5 1967, Perec observed that roughly between 1945 and 1955, there were two types of literature, one which was politically engaged and defended by Sartre and by Communist writers, and the other type which was the opposite, as it was apolitical: instead of fine sentiments, there were ugly opinions, instead of interesting stories about political and economic aspects of French society, there were stories about the relationship between a rich young man and a poor girl, and things of that sort. H. Coulet (ed.), *Idées sur le roman* (Paris: Larousse, 1992), 404.
2. J. Rousset, *Forme et signification. Essai sur les structures littéraires de Corneille à Claudel* (Paris: José Corti, 1961), ii.
3. It must be recognized that the genetic structuralism of Lucien Goldmann, the author of *Pour une sociologie du roman*, presents itself as an alliance between the sociology of the novel and the New Criticism, even though these two approaches would seem contradictory.

4. T. Todorov, *La littérature en peril* (2007), 31.
5. Translator's note : "Roman du moi" is a term coined by Michel Zink to describe a type of writing which first became widespread in French medieval literature, and which claimed to be the product of an individual consciousness. In this writing, contends Zink, "writers and poets, memorialists and historians, locate and define themselves and their subjects via the anecdotic moment, intimate, unshared". In other words, these were early examples of an authorial presence melded with a heterodiegetic narrator. See Jane M. Taylor, *The Poetry of François Villon: Text and Context* (Cambridge, UK: Cambridge University Press, 2001), 54.
6. P. Bayard, *Le plagiat par anticipation* (Paris: Minuit, 2009), 93.
7. T. S. Eliot, *To Criticize the Critic and Other Writings* (London: Faber & Faber, 1965), 18.
8. G. Steiner, *No Passion Spent*: Essays 1978–1996 (London and Boston: Faber and Faber), 1996, 203.
9. M. Robert, *Livre de lectures* (Paris: Grasset & Fasquelle, 1977), 137.
10. A. Finkielkraut, *The Defeat of the Mind*, 1995, translated by Judith Friedlander (NY: Columbia University Press), 120.
11. Ibid., 183.

CHAPTER 4

The Writer's Seductive Power

Abstract For those who love books, reading is a seductive affair between reader and writer. Fiction of any type undeniably brings mental pleasure to its readers. To write fiction is to speak to the other, with style and art. To review the writer's magic is to reveal that literary writing is like a declaration of love, a linguistic construct bent on seduction, as Freudians would attest. Desire, whether powerful or powerless, is present in not only the essence of the act of writing, in the very theme of the story, but also in the reader's horizon of expectations. This is why it is fruitful to bring a psychoanalytic approach to bear on reading literature.

Keywords Seduction • Fiction • Pleasure • Freud • Desire • Literature

> Seduction … is not of the order of the real and is never of the order of force, nor relations of force. But precisely for this reason, it enmeshes all power's *real* actions, as well as the entire reality of production, in this unremitting reversibility and dis-accumulation—*without which there would be neither power nor accumulation.*
>
> —Jean Baudrillard

I usually follow my heart when choosing what to read. To pause and consider this may seem commonplace or clinical, devoid of any overreaction, but this amorous encounter with the book is of the utmost importance. Indeed, I am increasingly convinced that the relationship of individuals to

© The Editor(s) (if applicable) and The Author(s) 2016

J.-F. Vernay, *The Seduction of Fiction*,
DOI 10.1007/978-3-319-39453-4_4

literature implies an underlying seductive enterprise between writer and reader. Seduction implies attraction, and attraction can be achieved by distraction (understood here as entertainment). This is one of the basic equations of literature which, in my eyes, allows the reader to give credence to the story. The writer is a professional at seduction who, by the medium of the narrator, uses and abuses the imaginary to secure the reader's belief. But how do fiction writers manage to seduce readers without hiding behind a mask, without producing a display of realistic fallacy? In postmodern works, especially, how do writers manage to charm the reader while simultaneously denouncing the artifice that causes seduction to occur? As the critic John Blair has highlighted, "… fiction exists thanks to an implicit contract between author and reader whereby the latter promises to give contemporary credence to an imitation world in return for *entertainment* and/or enlightenment."[1]

In analyzing Blair's syntax, it is obvious that distraction, part of the desire to appeal, comes first over any anxiety to educate the reader. The desire to appeal is often consubstantial with a *mimetic desire* that responds to a concern to strive for realism, to show the world as it is, unvarnished and without ornament. But then how is it that science fiction stories, which sometimes elude the mimetic desire, still manage to attract a wide readership? The answer may lie in the ability of fiction to provide psychic pleasure to readers through narrative techniques coupled with readers' own capacities for invention.

Let us keep in mind that a writer always writes for others, and those claiming to write for themselves are, according to Umberto Eco, "dishonest and lying narcissists. There is only one thing that you write for yourself, and that is a shopping list. It helps to remember what you have to buy, and when you have bought everything, you can destroy it, because it is no use to anyone else. Every other thing that you write, you write to say something to someone."[2] But telling is not enough. One needs to master the art of writing in order to be part of the literary tradition. In order to stimulate readers' emotions, the author displays a clear aesthetic ambition to which other objectives can be added. To gain hold of the reader, writers have at their disposal many spells or charms which they can decide to combine or not. In the case of author–narrator collusion, it is possible that this complicity be maintained by an unreliable narrator but who, nevertheless, highlights here and there some cracks in the truth in his own tale. In certain cases, readers are perfectly able to separate the narrator from the author because they cannot stop themselves from believing that the writer left discrete clues for them to be warned against the influence and the seduction of this unscrupulous narrator. It follows that readers, trapped in a fool's game, will be either embittered by a traitorous narrative twist or pushed to challenge their gullibility.

The writer can also provide a charming and illusory alternative world, its illusions carefully packaged, creating a veneer of truth that makes it credible. And despite the numerous metafictional references with which some tales are peppered, it is not unusual for authors to lure readers into their verbal constructions. Like expert salesmen, authors, in addition to stating what the reader wants to hear, can still wrap their messages in a poetic musicality that bewitches the most music-loving of readers. Whatever spells are used, authors seem to speak with forked tongues (authorial voice versus narrative voice)—a schizophrenic approach, even—creating some ambivalence in the reader. This ambivalence is expressed by constant oscillation in the minds of readers, now the victims of their "literary superstitions"[3] insofar as their suspension of disbelief[4] will enable fiction to seduce readers, now dismissing these literary superstitions as mere verbal matter and literary constructs.

The finding that the creative inspiration and the impulses of the heart are similar in that "both are higher actualizations of desire, of energy that moves us"[5] is somewhat of a cliché; but it must be admitted that Freud's intuition has largely contributed to turning the harmony between creativity and sexuality into a truism. On the one hand, in *Three Essays on the Theory of Sexuality* (1905), it is Freud's theory of the libido which makes sexual energy the bedrock of all human activity, while on the other hand, he advances the concept of sublimation, a process that realizes the mutation of the sexual drive (*Trieb*) into professions, especially artistic ones, "apparently unrelated to sex, but finding their aptitude in the force of sexual instinct."[6] In their frantic search for *libido sciendi* (desire for knowledge), certain literary critics such as Robert Scholes even had the audacity to pair creation and reproduction by identifying congruence between orgasmic and novelistic rhythms:

> The archetype of all fiction is the sexual act. … For what connects fiction … with sex is the fundamental orgiastic rhythm of tumescence and detumescence, of tension and resolution, of intensification to the point of climax and consummation. In the sophisticated forms of fiction, as in the sophisticated practice of sex, much of the art consists of delaying climax within the framework of desire in order to prolong the pleasurable act itself. When we look at fiction with respect to its form alone, we see a pattern of events designed to move toward climax and resolution, balanced by a counter-pattern of events designed to delay this very climax and resolution.[7]

Coitus interruptus.

Even Roland Barthes admits that desire is at the heart of the literary process at all levels—conception, reception, and interpretation. According to him, "to go from reading to criticism is to change desires; it is no longer to desire the work but to desire one's own language. But by that very process it is to send the work back to the desire to write from which it arose. And so discourse circulates around the book: reading, writing: all literature goes from one desire to the other."[8] Literary writing would therefore symbolize the passage from desire to the aesthetic, an intuition confirmed by Octave Mannoni, following psychoanalytic thinking.

> Freud's theory … might suggest that desire works like a technician hidden away from the real world. … Literature suggests that if the desire to write is a kind of sublimation of unconscious desire; it is not generally a complete sublimation, assuming such a thing exists, leaving lucent something non-sublimated in unconscious desire. In other words, the desire to write is also, if more obscurely, the desire to write about desire: fundamentally an impossible desire of writing about impossible desire. Writing has always contained, even if hidden, the trace of an unnameable desire.[9]

On a thematic level, representations of *libido sentiendi* (sensual desire) can vary according to the sex and sexuality of the writer who, if need be, can highlight the distinction between physiological desire and the fictional characters' feelings of love. The author may also evoke melancholy on the pages of the novel and, between the lines, explore ennui such as the one experienced in existential crises that "reveals the character of helpless desire." "The feeling of helplessness in ennui, felt as a lack of desire, overlaid by suffering, is more of an inhibition than a failure indicating, as in autism, the total withdrawal of the object."[10] Furthermore, a writer's own frustrations in the face of a society that he sees as unsatisfactory can trigger utopian impulses, namely the desire to fashion a perfect world which defeats the dissatisfactions of real life. Since literature is creation, and since fiction writing can be seen as a projection of the author's desire, the psychological investigation of the characters seems totally legitimate, something Roland Barthes would certainly not contradict.[11]

In some ways, literature also arises in response to the desire of readers, if I follow the strand of my framework borrowed from the aesthetic of reception; and this desire is embodied as much in the reader's "horizon of expectations" as in the need to interpret, derived from a need to share one's emotional response to aesthetics. As Wolfgang Iser points out,

"Perhaps this is the prime usefulness of literary criticism—it helps to make conscious those aspects of the text which would otherwise remain concealed in the subconscious; it satisfies (or helps to satisfy) our desire to talk about what we have read."[12] In this game of literary seduction, specular desire (the writer's desire that reflects the reader's) combines two fantasizing activities:

> The reader who is going to be shaped by the literary work starts off with *a kind of liaison*. Even during interruptions in the reading, while preparing to pick it up again, he abandons himself to the dream; his daydreaming is stimulated, he inserts fragments of it into the passages of the book, and *his reading is a hybrid*, a graft of his own fantasizing on the *fantasized works of the author*.[13]

It is clear that Didier Anzieu's reference to literary seduction in *Le corps de l'œuvre* (1981) (The body of the work), is modest support for the potential usefulness of psychoanalysis to my psycholiterary approach.

Notes

1. John G. Blair, *The Confidence Man in Modern Fiction* (London: Vision Press, 1979), 134. Emphasis added.
2. U. Eco, *On Literature*, 334.
3. Paul Valéry, seeking to define what he means by "literary superstitions," explains himself in these terms: "I call thus all beliefs that share the forgetfulness of the verbal condition of literature." P. Valéry, "Littérature" *Tel quel* (Paris: Gallimard, 1943), 162.
4. For the record, "this willing suspension of disbelief," of which Coleridge speaks, is the contract between the author and the reader by which the latter engages, playing the credulity card—not questioning the logic and reasonableness of narrative discourse. S.T. Coleridge, *Biographia Literaria*, (London: Dent & Sons Ltd, 1906 [1977]), 169. Genette sees this contract as being "the more or less tacit agreement of an audience that ... voluntarily renounces the right to object." *Fiction et diction* (Paris: Le Seuil, 1991), 51.
5. B. Cannone, *L'écriture du désir* (Paris: Calmann-Levy, 2000), 20.
6. J. Laplanche and J.-B. Pontalis, *Vocabulaire de la psychanalyse* (Paris: P.U.F., 1967), 465.
7. R. Scholes, *Fabulation and Metafiction* (Chicago: University of Illinois Press, 1979), 26.
8. R. Barthes, *Criticism and Truth*, translated and edited by Katrine Pilcher Keuneman (NY and London: Continuum, 2007/1966), 40.

9. O. Mannoni, *Clefs pour l'imaginaire*, 105.
10. M. Huguet, *L'ennui ou la douleur du temps* (Paris: Masson, 1987), 19–20.
11. R. Barthes, *Sur Racine* (Paris: Le Seuil, 1963).
12. W. Iser, in D. Lodge (ed.), *Modern Criticism and Theory: a Reader* (London and New York: Longman), 1988, 306.
13. D. Anzieu, *Le corps de l'œuvre* (Paris: Gallimard 1981), 45–46, emphasis added.

CHAPTER 5

The Symbiosis of Psychoanalysis and Fiction

Abstract Literature and psychoanalysis enjoy a symbiotic relationship; Freud himself emphasized the link between artistic creation, escapist fantasy and emotional involvement. The transposition of the real world into fictional space, in accordance with the creator's desire, is a process invested with emotion. Writers construct and enter imaginary spaces of representation where they can play roles by assuming characters, being fully responsible for the distribution of characters, which will lure the reader into identification or empathy. The reconciliation of psychoanalysis with the humanities is due not only to the literary skills of theoreticians such as Freud, Lacan, and others but also to strong affinities between Freudianism and fiction that are fully elaborated in this chapter.

Keywords Freud • Literature • Psychoanalysis • Escapism • Fantasy • Emotional involvement • Identification

> … since psychoanalytic theory and the literary text mutually inform—and displace—each other; since the very position of the interpreter—of the analyst—turns out to be not *outside*, but *inside* the text, there is no longer a clear-cut opposition or a well-defined border between literature and psychoanalysis: psychoanalysis could be intraliterary just as much as literature is intrapsychoanalytic. The methodological stake is no longer that of the application of psychoanalysis to literature, but rather of their interimplication in each other.
>
> —Shoshana Felman

© The Editor(s) (if applicable) and The Author(s) 2016

J.-F. Vernay, *The Seduction of Fiction*,
DOI 10.1007/978-3-319-39453-4_5

Stemming from a vast body of work of more than 6000 pages, Freud's legacy is felt all the more keenly in France, the most Freudian country in the world. I have had recourse to Freudian discourse on so many occasions in my work that I see literature and psychoanalysis as beneficent bedfellows; indeed, from the perspective of psycholiterary analysis, one cannot have enough of a discipline like psychoanalysis which has for so long willingly maintained affinities with the humanities. If we wish to reflect on the psychic mechanisms governing literary creation, the theories of Sigmund Freud and Didier Anzieu are indispensable. By opposing reality, literary creation becomes, to use Freud's hypothesis, a form of concealed fantasizing by way of the invention of a remarkable new world:

> Should we not look for the first traces of imaginative activity as early as in childhood? The child's best-loved and most intense occupation is with his play or games. Might we not say that every child at play behaves like a creative writer, in that he creates a world of his own, or, rather, re-arranges the things of his world in a new way which pleases him? It would be wrong to think he does not take that world seriously; on the contrary, he takes his play very seriously and he expends large amounts of emotion on it. The opposite of play is not what is serious but what is real.[1]

The transposition of the real world into fictional space, that seeks to reorder things in line with the creator's desire, is indeed invested, with "large amounts of emotion." Writing, like playfulness in childhood, allows subjects "free organization of the fantasies of their desire"[2] by giving them the possibility of make-believe in a transitional space where inner and outer worlds coexist. Like the child, the writer enters an imaginary space of representation where she or he can play a role by assuming a character as well as by being fully in charge of the cast of characters. In creating worlds in which reality is bent to match their objectives, writers or children can take pleasure in both creating and destroying. To cite Didier Anzieu, for whom the work of writing "fulfils a narcissistic desire for omnipotence":

> To be a novelist … is to infinitely shape at will,—even within inevitable limitations—the characters, situations, speeches, imaginary feelings. Writers are more comfortable with words than with people, as people and objects resist them while they make of interior images, and the impulses that propel them, what they want through the words that come to them—by way of a gift, or by their training, by this specific mixture of sudden inspiration and persistent work. They can thus invent at will a world (the story or picture of a single

> consciousness, a couple, a group) through to a whole society and its human comedy; and readers will enter this world in which they have been made to sufficiently believe, to move, and to be moved by it. The demiurgic omnipotence of the creator is therefore trans-narcissistic, as André Green has put it ... It is also transitional, as Winnicott intuitively expressed long ago.[3]

These days, with the assistance of computers, creative writers can endlessly create and destroy: The creator can thus escape the irreversibility and immutability of all production preserved through its worldly footprint. As Umberto Eco says in *On Literature*, the computer "encourages spontaneity: you dash down, in a hurry, whatever comes to mind ... [knowing] that later you can always correct and vary it."[4] But anyone seeing the computer as the basis of a spontaneous and magical conception of the novel would expose himself to the Bologna semiotician's caustic humor, of which I shall not deprive you:

> First of all you need a computer, obviously, which is an intelligent machine that thinks for you—and this would be an advantage for many people. All you need is a program of a few lines, even a child could do it. Then one feeds into the computer the content of a few hundred novels, scientific works, the Bible, the Koran, and many telephone directories (very useful for characters' names). Say, something like 120,000 pages. After this, using another program, you randomize, in other words, you mix all those texts together, making some adjustment, for instance eliminating all the *a*'s. Thus as well as a novel you would have a lipogram. At this point, you press "print" and it prints out. Having eliminated all the *a*'s, what comes out is something less than 120,000 pages. After you have read them carefully, several times, underlining the most significant passages, you load them onto an articulated truck and take them to an incinerator. Then you simply sit under a tree, with a piece of charcoal and good-quality drawing paper in hand, and allowing your mind to wander you write down a couple of lines. For instance, "The moon is high in the sky/the wood rustles." Maybe what emerges initially is not a novel but, rather, a Japanese haiku; nevertheless, the important thing is to get started.[5]

If literary creation appears to be a transient altered state of consciousness which encourages escapism and defers reality testing, writing could then be perceived as a quest for gratification, the fulfillment of which would make a fantasy world come true. Novelistic plot construction, as with the child's game, occupies a space at the intersection of affect and perception, of representation and expression, all proceeding from a projection mechanism. Philippe Gutton makes clear that "the phenomenon of projection is constant in the game of which it constitutes the fundamental mechanism ... This inward-outward movement inherent to spatial location constitutes the psychological basis of a certain number of definitions of projections."[6] This projection, occurring as a rush of freedom, is a way for the writer to escape from reality and avoid sources of unpleasure.

Literature is generally defined as a production of the mind, and psychoanalysis, to quote Charles Rycroft, can be defined as "mental anatomy."[7] Some consider these two domains to be so contiguous that their rivalry can be expressed in their common ability to illuminate understanding of the psychological motivations of the human being. The most radical critics willingly accuse psychoanalysis of being literature! But would it not be wiser to align with Paul-Lauren Assoun's view that Freud invented "some kind of new 'literary genre', psychoanalytic writing?"

Starting from the premise that literature and psychoanalysis form a symbiotic relationship that fueled Freud's work[8] between 1897 and 1928, I have undertaken an appraisal of this "interimplication," referred to by Shoshana Felman in the epigraph to this chapter. The problem was that for a long time, literature and psychoanalysis were seen as two disciplines quarreling about who should have a chair at the Collège de France.[9] Marthe Robert evokes this rivalry between the novelist and specialists of the psyche (including psychoanalysts) with great acuity:

> Generally speaking, psychology and the novel sustain a relationship that is poorly-defined. As the undisputed expert in affairs of the heart and all those who more or less depend on it, novelists feel deep down that their profession is highly superior to that of psychologists who, luckily, are too convinced of novelists' incompetence in this field to risk debunking this view. Having received the gracious gift of penetrating souls and making what they discover into a perfect apparition of interiority, novelists show little interest in acquiring more knowledge in this area; or if they do manage to look more closely, it is not to put more effort into ways to augment, amplify or authenticate their characters and conflicts, but at most to enrich their cast of characters with that of a psychologist or psychiatrist whose narrow mind and impotence are most often used as a foil to the deep-souled hero (never is this character so badly treated as in the form of the psychoanalyst figure ...).[10]

Freud demonstrated, with the controversial case of Dr. Daniel Paul Schreber, that we can examine the psyche of subjects without automatically putting them on a couch. Having said this, critics should be no more inclined to make a diagnosis than to put authors on a couch. So let there be no mistake about it: Just as the critics' line of duty is to analyze how authors couch their words, so literary criticism must not allow the critics to turn authors into analysands by inviting them to lie down on the couch, no matter how comfortable this couch might be! Perhaps the critic's task is to find out to what extent the characters or the heroes are modeled on sensible psychological patterns with the view of construing this technique as an additional "reality effect" (what Roland Barthes has termed "effet de réel"), which spins readers into a greater delusional web of identification and empathy with the characters.

It is not my intention to discuss the validity of psychoanalysis, but I want to clarify that we can and must challenge Freud, because it is up to all of us—especially an informed reader—to exercise this "right of examination,"[11] to make sense of things. But to reject totally this system of thought would be regrettable, and all the more so nowadays when psychoanalysis is rightly associated more with literature and philosophy than it is with psychiatry or psychology. This reconciliation with the humanities is due not only to the literary verve and rhetorical skill of theoreticians such as Freud himself and others such as Jacques Lacan, Françoise Dolto, Bruno Bettelheim, and Serge Leclaire, but also to the real affinities between Freudianism and fiction, beyond alliteration, which I am now going to enumerate.

The question is no longer that of the application of psychoanalysis to literature, but rather, of their interimplication. With his 1907 essay entitled *Delusions and Dreams in Jensen's Gradiva*, Freud laid the foundation stone for the monument of psychoanalysis and its built-in bridges leading on to fiction, of which Roland Barthes speaks in *The Pleasure of the Text* (1973); he asserts it is a monument that "must be traversed, not bypassed, like the fine thoroughfares of a very large city, across which we can play, dream, etc.: a fiction."[12] Thanks to this seminal interimplication of psychoanalysis and fiction, Freud paved the way for more extended psychoanalytic treatment of literature by international scholars such as Bruno Bettelheim, Marie Bonaparte, Janine Chasseguet-Smirgel, André Green, Jacques Lacan, Charles Mauron, Otto Rank, Marthe Robert, to name a few; and not forgetting Jean Bellemin-Noël who propounded his "textanalysis" (la textanalyse) concept for the first time in the early 1980s. In *La psychanalyse du texte littéraire* (1996), Jean Bellemin-Noël posits that "all texts are influenced by unconscious forces which can be observed and described."[13]

The critics should therefore listen to what the text is telling them by reading between the lines, by paying attention to what is left unsaid by the characters, by interpreting the various settings, by reading into the polysemy of words, by examining what is implied behind the figures of speech, and so on. To be sure, it would be painstakingly tricky to contend that textanalysis is not another way of couching "applied psychoanalysis" but this supports the notion that Freudianism and fiction can only benefit from each other.

For me, fiction and psychoanalysis, both aiming at coming to a greater understanding of the human mind, have expanded along the same lines. Both claim that there is a surface meaning (the text/the ego) and a richer or more telling under-the-surface-meaning (the subtext/the superego and the id). Both have witnessed how discourse has superseded man with the revolutionary teachings of the New Criticism when structuralist Barthes audaciously proclaimed "the death of the author" (*la mort de l'auteur*), and then of post-Freudian psychoanalysis when post-structuralist Jacques Lacan contended that "The unconscious is structured like a language." But it so happens that earlier on Freud took another line by suggesting the existence of a closer link between novelists and their literary creations.

In "Creative Writers and Day-Dreaming," Freud believed in the capacity of psychological novelists, who cared to go through self-observation, to split up their egos "into many part-egos," with those parts being projected onto several characters—characters he generically termed "heroes." These part-egos could be seen to epitomize the "conflicting currents" of the writer's mental life. If Freud was actually referring to novels, a stumbling block would arise from New Criticism, a school of thought for which the writer—*Homo sapiens*—is to be clearly dissociated from the character—*Homo fictus*. If we are dealing with life stories, with the exception of heterobiographies (the term coined by Philippe Lejeune for the life story of a person written by another person), it is another matter altogether because the writer and the literary subject at the core of autobiographies are purportedly one. Now if writers are indeed able to diffract their personality into their own literary creations, readers exploring the psychological underpinnings of a work of fiction should be entitled to read into the various characters some of the author's personality traits—at least on a theoretical level. The sad fact is that unless anyone personally knows a creative writer to the point of disentangling facts from fictions, such a venture will be both pointless and fruitless.

In the case of both fiction and psychoanalysis, one needs to dig into the substrata of the surface layers to unearth the hidden messages, be they of creative writers or of the unconscious. In a nutshell, both fields share a definite common ground which covers the resonating power of language, rhetoric, affects, the readable subject, the mind, intimacy linked to scopophilia, and similar structures. They both use words not only for what they denote, but also, more importantly, perhaps, for what they connote. Their discourse is fraught with affectively charged thoughts which facilitate the processes of identification in literature and of transference in psychoanalytic practice. The readable subject which is at the core of both disciplines is deconstructed as a body of words which needs to be interpreted, a body of signs which needs to be deciphered, and a body of sounds which needs to be carefully listened to. For the arts, the mind fuels the imagination, "the unconsciousness of the unconscious"—as Roland Barthes defines it in *The Pleasure of the Text*—whereas, the mind in psychoanalysis is the seat of the conscious and the unconscious. The voyeuristic analyst and critic seem to share the same scopophilic drives through their invasion of intimacy by prying into dark secrets, or is it the other way around? The analysand and writer are becoming shameless exhibitionists through the display of their intimacy. As for similar structures, the psychoanalytic interpretation of dreams does parallel the basic architectonics of fiction with the division between the manifest and the latent content which can be transposed in literary terms as the text and subtext, by the condensation and displacement mechanisms in the primary process corresponding to the operative functions of figures of speech like metaphor and metonymy, not to mention dream images which find an echo in surrealism, magic realism, fantasy, science fiction, realism, and naturalism.

To adequately interpret a discourse, both psychoanalysts and literary critics need to analyze how words are couched. Ultimately, both of them become a sort of Sherlock Holmes in interpreting their material. Enamored of Arthur Conan Doyle stories, Freud brought into synergy the investigative work of the psychoanalyst with that of the detective when he approached the question of parapraxis in *The Psychopathology of Everyday Life* (1901). To put words on the couch, it is necessary to impersonate a skillful detective in search of conclusive evidence—to borrow a famous Freudian metaphor:

> "And if you were a detective engaged in tracing a murder, would you expect to find that the murderer had left his photograph behind at the place of the crime, with his address attached? Or would you not necessarily have to be satisfied with comparatively slight and obscure traces of the person you were in search of? So do not let us underestimate small indications; by their help we may succeed in getting on the track of something bigger."[14]

Lacan, in his comment on Poe's "The Purloined Letter,"[15] and Lacanian philosopher Slavoj Zizek in "The Detective and the Analyst" (1990)[16] have notoriously taken up the analogy to this investigative method, a method which requires a keen eye for detail. As clues need to be conclusive, the critic ought to come up with a body of evidence—what French law terms *un faisceau de preuves*. A few isolated pointers stretched to fit a larger pattern would obviously be tantamount to tacking psychoanalytic concepts onto literary texts. Needless to specify that far-fetched interpretations are not the prerogative of psychoanalytic criticism as they stand for the classic pitfalls of literary criticism.

Among the opponents of the power of psychoanalysis was hospital psychiatrist Jean Cottraux, a strong participant in the demystifying project of *The Black Book of Psychoanalysis* (2005), asserting that "psychoanalysis is a form of art as it plays on illusion, suggestion, and a function of the human mind which consists in filling in the blanks of perception by interpretations."[17] This was something Freud never tried to hide, avowing in his own words that psychoanalysis, just as much as literary criticism, was "an art of interpretation." Upon reflection, the detractors of psychoanalysis end up doing the humanities a big favor: The more they seek to repudiate the scientific nature of psychoanalysis, the more the symbiotic relationship between psychoanalysis and fiction is revealed!

Notes

1. S. Freud, "Creative Writers and Day-Dreaming" in Peter Gay (ed.), *The Freud Reader* (NY and London: Norton, 1989), 437.
2. "To have, to lose, to do and undo, and redo differently, to create, uncreate, recreate indefinitely our relationships with people and things, this is what always seems new and fascinating in the endlessly renewed games humans play in search of our pleasure, and our self-conquests. Searching also for mastery of the reality of nature, of the society of which the human is always at once contributor and object. It is the free organization of fantasies of his desires that he wants to make a game of, without too much risk, to find his pleasure and to share it with his fellow humans." F. Dolto, *Les étapes majeures de l'enfance* (Paris: Gallimard, 1994), 121.
3. D. Anzieu, *Créer, détruire* (Paris: Dunod, 1996), 37.
4. U. Eco, *On Literature*, 332.
5. Ibid., 330–331.
6. P. Gutton, *Le jeu chez l'enfant: essai psychanalytique* (Paris: Larousse, 1973), 38.

7. C. Rycroft, *Psychoanalysis and Beyond* (London: Chatto & Windus, 1985), 268.
8. Freud, a dedicated bibliophile who certainly had excellent writing skills, such that he was awarded the Goethe prize for Literature in 1930, is well known for providing readers with subtle and original readings of literary texts such as *Hamlet* and *The Merchant of Venice*. Greatly inspired by literature in general, he was intellectually stimulated by authors like Dostoevsky, Conan Doyle, Goethe, Hoffmann, Jensen, Sophocles, Shakespeare, Ovid and Zweig, not to mention the range of writers he quoted in *Jokes and Their Relation to the Unconscious* (1905), and the scores of allusions to *The Bible* in his work.
9. Translator's note: The *Collège de France* is a renowned research and educational institution in Paris where university professors give regular free lectures to the public.
10. M. Robert, *Livre de lectures*, 154–155.
11. J. Cottraux, in C. Meyer (ed.), *Le livre noir de la psychanalyse* (Paris: Les arènes, 2005), 257.
12. R. Barthes, *The Pleasure of the Text*, translated by Richard Miller (New York: Hill and Wang, 1975), 31.
13. J. Bellemin-Noël, *La psychanalyse du texte littéraire* (Paris: Nathan, 1996), 75.
14. S. Freud (1916–1917): "Introductory Lectures on Psycho-Analysis," in: Sigmund Freud, *The Standard Edition of the Complete Psychological Works* (London: Hogarth Press. Vol. 15 & 16, 1963), 27.
15. J. Lacan, Seminar on "The Purloined Letter," translated by Jeffrey Mehlman, *Yale French Studies*, 48 (1973), 39–72.
16. S. Zizek. "The detective and the analyst," *Literature and Psychology*, 36 (1990), 27–46.
17. J. Cottraux in C. Meyer (ed.), *Le livre noir*, 195.

CHAPTER 6

The Art of Storytelling

Abstract Building on Todorov's view that literature opens the possibility of interaction with others that can infinitely enrich us, this chapter shows how emotions engendered in us by literature can give our real world more sense. Since the eighteenth century, the novel has tried to reproduce plausible events in the real world in order to construct "possible worlds" that seem so real that readers feel they could live in them. The myth-making property of our brains is thus stimulated by the superimposition of facts and fiction, which lies at the heart of storytelling.

Keywords Emotions • Feelings • Imagination • Psychoanalysis • Myth-making

> The old biographer's problem: even when people are telling their own life stories, they are invariably improving on the facts, rewriting their tales, or just plain making them up.
>
> —Salman Rushdie

The supreme contribution of psychoanalysis has been to put us "on the path of a fundamental aspect of consciousness: the fabricating function, the propensity of consciousness to fabricate myths—stories by and about oneself,"[1] according to French neurologist Lionel Naccache. In considering "literature as licensed fabrication,"[2] Freudian theorist Marthe Robert was in perfect accord with neuroscientific theories that view the imagina-

© The Editor(s) (if applicable) and The Author(s) 2016

J.-F. Vernay, *The Seduction of Fiction*,
DOI 10.1007/978-3-319-39453-4_6

tion and reality as having a privileged relationship. More recently, French psychiatrist Roland Jouvent argues that "if reality is completely satisfying we can totally abandon ourselves to it. But if instead the environment is displeasing, our imagination comes to occupy our thoughts, to avoid dwelling on such negative reality."[3] Is it overstating the case to suggest that each and every one of us has the potential to become a compulsive storyteller?

Psychiatrists have it that storytelling, while considered normal in children, becomes pathological in adults, precisely because fantasizing is the art of portraying imagined deeds as if they were real. Without encroaching too much on the following chapter, I would say that the novelistic art of plot-making and fabrication can be summed up in three words: demonstration, diction, and invention. The latter derives from the Latin *inventio*, meaning "discovery," offered in the first place to its creator, a notion that inspired Milan Kundera to write that "by inventing his novel, the novelist discovers a hitherto unknown aspect of 'human nature'; a novelist's invention is therefore an act of knowledge …",[4] just as much as an act of acknowledgement of reality. For as the Czech writer recalls: "'Prose': the word signifies not only a nonversified language; it also signifies the concrete, everyday, corporeal nature of life. So to say that a novel is the art of prose is not to state the obvious; the word defines the deep sense of that art."[5]

Literature and imagination appear as two overlapping areas in the shared zone of possibilities and to believe a good number of enthusiastic writers, this licensed fabrication would not have any other purpose than to reveal humans to themselves (following Kundera's argument above) or to others, let alone to the entire world! In an interview with Christian Salmon, Kundera asserts that, "a novel examines not reality, but existence. And existence is not what has occurred, it is the realm of human possibilities, everything that man can become, everything he's capable of."[6]

As for Tzvetan Todorov, "literature opens up infinitely this possibility of interaction, and thus inestimably enriches us. It provides us with fundamental feelings that make the real world seem more beautiful, more charged with meaning. Far from being mere pleasure, a distraction reserved for the educated, reading fiction makes each of us more human."[7] But if the novel interprets life before the reader has even interpreted the novel, would not this *mise en abyme* be hazardous and lead to overinterpretation, to an overexploitation of the imagination, to unrealistic ideas, even distortion of the truth? We are thus approaching the very essence of invention.

In his book *Fiction and Diction*, Genette states that it is impossible to suggest a formal demarcation between fiction and factual representation. Since the eighteenth century, the novel has sought to replicate the real world and plausible events in order to construct so-called "possible worlds" that seem so true we could live in them. These borrowings from the real certainly contribute to the fluidity of reading; for, in the absence of thorough documentation, it is a safe bet that the Model Reader would stumble on any inaccurate information provided by the author. Readers are thus turned into inhabitants living on the littoral of both imaginary and real homelands. Therein lies the trap set by the subgenres such as fictional biography and autobiography, realist or naturalist novels, and roman à clef or historical novels, all of which flirt dangerously with the real to the point of seducing readers into a greater delusional web of identification and empathy with the characters. Moreover, realism clearly poses the problem of the ambiguous relationship between what is of the factual order of reality, as it is lived by humans, and what is of the imaginary order, namely fabrication derived from mental constructs generated by the human brain.

The superimposition of fact and fiction, often perceived as detrimental to the literary work because it calls into question the creative capacities of the author, also seems to demonstrate that creation *ex nihilo* (out of nothing) is an illusory concept. According to Mikhail Bakhtin's concept of dialogism, the logos (or discourse) of the author is shaped in dialogic interaction with a preceding logos, reinforcing the idea that the creative process involves an act of recomposition and reconstruction, all while steering a diffluent imagination that could thwart the aesthetic ambitions of trends like realism or naturalism.

The (post) modern trend, meanwhile, seeks to avoid if not to destroy the referential illusion that encourages the reader to give credence to the story. Viewed from this angle, more than a safety valve in the face of the constraints of realism, the inclusion of metafictional asides (which recognize the artificiality of realism conventions while simultaneously using them) delivers a clear message: The novel is more a linguistic construct than a slice of life!

There are some who think this licensed fabrication is condemned to be expressed within a restricted or even coercive framework. This is the view, in any case, of the OuLiPo Collective (an acronym for *Ouvoir de littérature potentielle*—"the workshop of potential literature"—a French literary group):

> Any literary work is constructed from an inspiration (at least, this is what authors would have us believe), that is somehow required to accommodate a series of constraints and procedures that fit one inside the other like Russian dolls: constraints of vocabulary and grammar, of structural rules of the novel (for example, division into chapters), or of the classical tragedy (the rule of three entities), constraints of general versification, and the fear of fixed forms (as in the case of the cycle or the sonnet), and so on.[8]

Because literary creation chimes so perfectly with imagination, there are many who think like Roland Barthes that the rules of writing and composition in literature are best subverted:

> Lastly, the text can, if it wants, attack the canonical structures of the language itself (Sollers): lexicon (exuberant neologisms, portmanteau words, transliterations), syntax (no more logical unit, no more sentence). It is a matter of effecting, by transmutation (and no longer only by transformation), a new philosophic state of the language-substance; this extraordinary state, this incandescent metal, outside origin and outside communication, then becomes language, and not a language, whether disconnected, mimed, mocked.[9]

Whatever the case, the writer is forced to give free reign to his imagination because, to reprise Fernando Pessoa's words, "Literature, like all art, is a confession that life is not enough."[10] Certainly, literature tries to outdo reality in creativity, but let there be no mistake about it, as William James said, "the concept 'dog' does not bite!"[11]

Notes

1. L. Naccache, "La conscience révélée," *Philosophie magazine* 36, February 2010, 76.
2. M. Robert, *Livre de lectures,* 147.
3. R. Jouvent, *Le cerveau magicien. De la réalité au plaisir psychique* (Paris: Odile Jacob, 2009), 11. Translator's note: this title translates as "The wizard brain: from reality to psychic pleasure."
4. M. Kundera, *The Curtain: An Essay in Seven Parts* (Harper Perennial; Reprint edition, 2007), 8.

5. Ibid., 8.
6. M. Kundera, *L'art du roman* (Paris: Gallimard, 1986), 61. This translation of the quote is cited in M. Mair, *Towards a Radical Redefinition of Psychology: The selected works of Miller Mair* [electronic resource] (Hoboken: Taylor and Francis, 2014), 129.
7. T. Todorov, *La littérature en peril*, 16.
8. OuLiPo, *La littérature potentielle* (Paris: Gallimard, 1973), 16.
9. R. Barthes, *The pleasure of the text*, translated by Richard Miller (New York: Hill and Wang, 1975), 31.
10. Cited in B. Cannone, *L'écriture du désir*, 123.
11. W. James, *Some Problems of Philosophy* (Cambridge, Mass.: Harvard University Press, 1979), 48.

CHAPTER 7

The Novel as a Work of Bad Faith

Abstract In fabricating a novel, writers are presenting as real what they know is untrue. Yet it must seem true enough to lure readers, and to seduce them into believing that the work conforms to reality. A large part of this is achieved by the Aristotelian principle of fictional mimesis, the representation of action, which Vernay subdivides into several strands, including illusory representation or "illusionism," and anti-illusionism or anti-representation, which draws attention to the fictionality of the text. Simultaneously, the writer must improve on the real through displacement in the manner of the Freudian primary purpose. To attempt to connect the real with fiction (the oxymoronic concept of 'true lies') is therefore futile: The very essence of the novel renders impossible all quests for truth.

Keywords Aristotle • Mimesis • Representation • Fictionality • Freud • "True lies"

> In literature, the word man no longer has two feet, only one foot. Those who give it two, that's their business, the writer isn't responsible. There's no such thing as the writer's responsibility. And as for guilt, even less so.[1]
>
> —Christine Angot

One might think that the reality effect would be obsolete in an image society now dominated by the audiovisual, but that is not the case. To write fiction is still at least in part to depict. To write is to offer a universe

© The Editor(s) (if applicable) and The Author(s) 2016

J.-F. Vernay, *The Seduction of Fiction*,
DOI 10.1007/978-3-319-39453-4_7

of representations which capture readers' imaginations, through the interpretive efforts of the brain.[2] I would also add that poetry and drama are at an advantage when compared to the novel in that they are less concerned with representing the exterior world. But the novel cannot escape it. To write is not to transcribe, and one must leave behind "the naive conception of a novelist as 'recorder' or 'stenographer' of reality"[3]; for if contemporary novelists are still deliberately seeking to make their works real, in the sense of plausible, they do not, for all that, claim to create reality.

For Michel Raimond, here acknowledging Maurice Blanchot, "the novel is a work of bad faith: the novelist presents as real what he knows to be untrue, and the reader pretends to take for real what he never forgets is fictitious."[4] The dictionary definition of the novel is "*fabricated* story, written in prose, in which the author seeks to excite interest through the depiction of passions and mores, or through the singularity of the adventures."[5] I emphasize the term "fabricated" for beyond the fact expressed by this adjective, there are connotations of trickery and concealment with which the novel is associated. It is precisely because "to make true therefore consists of making a complete illusion of the real" that Guy de Maupassant, in the preface of *Pierre et Jean*, recognizes realist writers as "illusionists."[6] The very fact that writers *want to make* it real proves beyond a doubt that it *is not* real, thus casting doubts on the plausibility of the novel.

Whether plausibility is understood as the confrontation of the fictional world with reality, or as the confrontation of an individual's representation (the viewpoint of a person) with a collective representation (the constructs of public opinion),[7] it is a lure contrived for the reader, a lure which aims at giving a deceptive impression of truth. By means of the lure, readers are trapped into believing that the work conforms to reality by its strong adherence to the truth of facts in order to fabricate historicity with much specific detail; while it is writers who, by means of literary constructs, bend reality to *their* designs, setting the directions they wish to assign to both history and their own stories. As emphasized by Michel Raimond, Emeritus Professor of contemporary literature at the Sorbonne, "one does not read a novel as one would an encyclopedia." He adds:

> So anxious were they to be a doctor of social science, the novelists of the last century never forgot they should first of all grab the reader's attention. Even when Zola, in his theoretical writings, claimed to renounce "the

construction of plot", and to present only "slices of life" or "human documents", he kept the practice of solicitously providing a progression of events to hold the reader spellbound. From Balzac to Zola, the novel often presents a dramatic structure, revealing a conflict based on plot details, and on the clash of characters or their ambitions. The observation of the real, in itself, does not produce a captivating story.[8]

What applies to novelists of realism, such as Balzac, Flaubert, the Goncourt brothers, Stendhal or Zola, also applies to other novelists like Australian Christopher Koch[9] whose realistic techniques reflect his concern for the accuracy of every little detail as much as it does his desire to trap the reader in a dramatic intensity that gives rhythm to a finely crafted, events-packed narrative.

It was Aristotle who formulated the principle of fiction according to which *poiesis* (i.e., the fabrication of works of art) implies *mimesis*, namely "imitation," or more precisely the representation of action. This representation essentially comes in two strands. One which I would define as *hetero*-representation, which in its turn is subdivided into two: The first of these is illusory representation, or "illusionism," Coetzee's term for illusory representation in which realistic writers are very accomplished; and "anti-illusionism," Coetzee's word for *anti*-representation, namely fiction which draws attention to the fictionality of the text no matter how representational it appears to be.[10] The second strand is called *auto-representation*. Camille Dumoulié sees in this Aristotelian heritage a novelistic aim which reveals itself in these terms:

… fiction will come to fill the supposed gap between the sign and its referent, between writing and things. Having recourse to the novel is what permits this demand to be met, less by the story and the mimesis of human actions, which are still often subject to the principles of conventional representation, than by descriptions aimed at presenting the real itself. This is however by means of a literary ruse that, in its suggestive 'depictions', offers a feigned, fictitious presence. The novel nevertheless pulls this off: it excites the desire for the real and the true that is produced imaginatively in the act of reading, finding expression through visualization.[11]

Whatever intentions we ascribe to the novel, we do not demand that it be true, only plausible, if it hopes to situate itself within realist or naturalistic traditions. Unlike journalism, fiction does not purport to be a faithful transcription of reality. Literary representations of persons who have historically existed are therefore not imitations of these people, since the words attributed to them do not directly relate to any speech uttered in real life. That is to say, the linguistic abilities of literary characters are engendered in an act of ventriloquism orchestrated by the novelist. And if by chance someone asks, "How do you know all about these events that you have never witnessed? By what right do you reproduce conversations that you never heard?," the novelist can answer with the panache of François Mauriac: "In truth, I have outlived most of my heroes including several who held a great place in my life."[12]

Yet according to another argument, the language of literature is devoid of extralinguistic reality, as we have been reminded by Gérard Cordesse, Gérard Lebas, and Yves le Pellec in their literary handbook. If the linguistic sign ordinarily refers to a referent (when something is said, it is effective because it exists or occurs in reality), it is quite another matter in the fictional universe where the "reference to an absent referent is characteristic of literary discourse whose referent is *always* imaginary."[13]

If the role of the professional reader is to uncover and reveal the tricks that helped the author construct the illusion, the non-professional reader's role is to be taken in by the illusory representation, known as the realistic fallacy. But professional readers can effectively be ensnared by a perverse effect: In seeking to shed light on the realistic illusion, to the extent of uncovering inconsistencies and anachronisms in the fictional narrative, they are exposing their own susceptibilities to the influence of fiction, which—I suppose—will dumbfound many readers! While the author labors only to embed the reader in a fictive, constructed reality, by way of techniques of verisimilitude, certain readers are being led astray, taking the fictional narrative at face value, up to the point of initiating legal disputes. Such disputes result from taking literary representations as true, a misunderstanding of the whole concept of literature.

The novel, through its filtering of representations, offers a mediation of reality, especially when it is a reality that could displease or offend. Literary representations of sexuality, for example, have long been portrayed euphemistically for fear that texts will be branded as indecent or pornographic and be subject to censorship. When it is not a literary interpretation of reality—"a reality represented, thought out, put into perspective, and illuminated with some meaning"[14]—the representation seen from another angle can be understood as a *re*-presentation, as a *new* (over)compensated presentation of a reality which some deem too dull, to the extent that borrowing from the real is just not enough for novelists.

They must improve on it through displacement or condensation in the manner of the Freudian primary process. Without inspiration, or dramatic interest, without a disguised reality, a novelist can hardly pique readers' interest, nor distract them from their dreary routines. The novelist's first task, then, is to create a perfect "imaginary world which [...] glimmers like a mirage, because the distinctive feature of the imaginary is to be relieved of the ordinary weight of things and of the monotony of daily life."[15]

Sometimes, and on such occasions a writer will go to great lengths to declare it to all and sundry, a book becomes a source of inspiration for people. But this collusion between the story and the reader masks the treacherous power of representation, a representation which, due to its particular orientation, is a highly subjective evocation of reality. For if one takes into account all the aspects of the life of the book, right from its first release, it seems to me that these representations which claim to dissect and examine society, come to wield influence by their very privileging of certain models of thought, behavior, *modus vivendi*, even sexuality, thus tempting readers into emulating these ideas in their own lives.

But just because everything in the novel is a matter of representation does not mean that one must repudiate the psychological dimension of fictional characters on the grounds that—even if they are representative of humankind—they remain "paper beings" (Paul Valéry).[16] Some authors construct stories consonant with a psychological approach manifested in characterization, including characters' motivations shown through their actions in the fictional space. Fictional writing that is approached as a projection of the author's desire can legitimize the search for psychological motivations of characters, without running the risk of confusing *Homo fictus* with *Homo sapiens.*

Literary representations appear as much as intrusions of the real in fiction (from the point of view of writing) as irruptions of the fictitious in the real (in terms of reading). But if one pushes this theoretical reflection, the fictitious and the real seem to return to their rightful places in the game of representation. As Jean Bessière points out in his introduction to his theoretical work on the novel *Roman, réalités, réalismes, "the real dissolves in fiction as fiction in the real".* So to seek the "intersection of the imaginary and the real"[17] and to attempt to connect the real with fiction, as Louis Aragon did with his oxymoronic concept of "true lies,"[18] is therefore futile: The very essence of the novel would seem to render impossible all quests for truth.

Notes

1. Angot, Christine, *Une partie du cœur* (Paris: Editions Stock, 2004). Kindle edition.
2. "When we read a novel, countless tiny intellectual operations occur continuously: while the eye scans the lines, the mind continues to register information … Furthermore, nothing is freer than an individual's imagination: from the same words, each reader conjures different images." M. Raimond, *Le roman*, 7.
3. Ibid., 54.
4. Ibid., 6.
5. Translator's note: The dictionary from which this definition was obtained, for the original French edition of this book, is the *Dictionnaire de la langue française* by Émile Littré, commonly called the "Littré," and the translation of the definition here is almost literal, except for the translation of the French word *feinte*; while this can mean feigned, or non-genuine (Collins Robert French-English Dictionary), the French word also has the connotation of deception, or a ruse or trap (Larousse Dictionary) and no similar English term can fully convey this. Thus, the word "fabricated" was selected for the English translation.
6. "'Truth' in such work consists in producing a complete illusion by following the common logic of facts and not by transcribing them pell-mell, as they succeed each other. Whence I conclude that the higher order of Realists should rather call themselves Illusionists." Guy de Maupassant, "Of the novel," Preface to de Maupassant, *Pierre & Jean*, translated by Clara Dell (New York: P. Collier, 1902), ii–iii.
7. *See* G. Cordesse, G. Lebas and Y. Le Pellec, *Langages littéraires: textes d'anglais,* especially "Le vraisemblable dans le roman", 79–104.
8. M. Raimond, *Le roman*, 53.
9. For further commentary on Koch, see J.-F. Vernay, *Water from the Moon: Illusion and Reality in the Works of Australian Novelist Christopher Koch* (NY: Cambria Press, 2007).
10. J. M. Coetzee, *Doubler le cap. Essais et entretiens* (Paris: Le Seuil, 2007), 24.
11. C. Dumoulié, *Littérature et philosophie* (Paris: Armand Colin, 2002), 119.
12. F. Mauriac cited in M. Raimond, *Le roman*, 123.
13. G. Cordesse, G. Lebas and Y. Le Pellec, *Langages littéraires*, 83. The full quotation is as follows: "Most of the time we talk about things in their absence rather than in their presence. To say 'the man I met this morning' is to point to a referent in absentia, that we shall attempt 'to evoke', to make 'present by using a definite description, identifying, qualifying, and so on. This reference to an absent referent is characteristic of literary discourse whose referent is always imaginary."

14. M. Raimond, *Le roman*, 10.
15. Ibid., 8.
16. P. Bayard, *Books You Haven't Read*, 16. As the author correctly points out: "Breaking with that critical tradition, Valéry posited that despite appearances an author is in no position to explain his own work. The work is the product of a creative process that occurs in the writer but transcends him, and it is unfair to reduce the work to that act of creation. To understand a text, therefore, there is little point in gathering information about the author, since in the final analysis he serves it only as a temporary shelter."
17. J. Bessière (ed.), *Roman, réalités, réalismes* (Paris: PUF, 1989), 7.
18. Translator's note: Louis Aragon (1897–1982) was a celebrated French intellectual, prolific fiction writer, poet, journalist, member of the French Resistance during World War II, and long-time member of the Communist Party. His concept of *le mentir-vrai*, outlined in his book of the same name, can be translated as "to lie truthfully" or "true lies," and has generated much varied commentary. For just two examples, see I. Wall, "The mentir-vrai and Aragon's politics", *The Romantic Review*, January 2001; and J. Kristeva, Chap. 6, "Aragon, defiance and deception: a precursor?" in *The sense and non-sense of revolt: the powers and limits of psychoanalysis*, trans. Jeanine Herman (New York: Columbia University Press, 2000).

CHAPTER 8

The Impossible Quest for Truth

Abstract Some readers still expect the novel to provide revelations, or truth, thinking perhaps that if art is not "truth," it must be lies. But fiction cannot be associated with mendacity in the novel because it is storytelling that has no intention to deceive, and is not subject to truth valuations. This is because the novel is a space that disallows a quest for truth. Instead, we have the fictional pact, in which the writer deceives and the reader willingly accepts the deception by suspension of disbelief. This leads to the central reflection: How can readers be moved emotionally by something they know does not exist?

Keywords Storytelling • Novel • Fictional pact • Suspension of disbelief

> Fiction is the lie through which we tell the truth.
>
> —Albert Camus

In discussing literature, one must include metaphysical aspects, for literature is about the function and nature of language, about the appearance of things, the fluidity between being and seeming, the capacity to fix reality (if one subscribes to the doctrine of universal mobilism, the notion of all things being in a constant state of flow and change), the questioning of the

© The Editor(s) (if applicable) and The Author(s) 2016

J.-F. Vernay, *The Seduction of Fiction*,
DOI 10.1007/978-3-319-39453-4_8

confrontation between the real and the imaginary, and so on. In opposition to the idea that language is no representation but a performative utterance which impacts on the real world, we can argue that in literature, representations are formed by a "shadow language,"[1] and that fiction is thus neither more nor less than reflections of reality (as in the myth of Plato's cave), or of what passes for reality in the actual world.

Against all common sense, some readers still expect the novel to provide revelations, not to mention truth (understood here as a definite principle, which holds all doubt in check). At the most basic level, these readers are perhaps "fearful that if art isn't 'true', it is a 'lie', as Plato in violence called it. Imaginative literature is a 'fiction', an artistic, verbal 'imitation of life'. The opposite of 'fiction' is not 'truth' but 'fact' or 'time-and-space existence.'"[2] Yet too few readers challenge the cliché that "good literature knows how to lie, that is to say, it knows how to invent a fictive world that makes the real world seem wanting."[3]

If there is indeed a lexical kinship between lying and fictional literature that exists as much in English as it does in French, which is inherent in the term fiction, fictional writing cannot be associated with mendacity in the novel genre, at least not on a philosophical level. In its archaic sense, the word fiction denotes a lie, while in the language of contemporary literature, it denotes a work of imagination; a similarity we see in English as evidenced by the denotations for fiction in the *Oxford English Dictionary*.[4] Common sense would indicate, then, that we heed the opinion of Peter McCormick when he says that "storytelling, unlike lying, is pretending without the intention to deceive, a storytelling more like charades than perjury."[5] He adds that "the writer of fiction … pretends to refer because the nature of fictional sentences is such that he or she cannot refer. The writer of a nonfictional work in using nonfictional sentences intends to refer; by contrast, the writer of a fictional work only pretends to refer."[6] In his explanation, distinguishing between non-fiction and fiction, McCormick implies that the notion of truth (which must henceforth be understood as "what is real," and more precisely as "consistent with fact or reality," as in the Oxford English Dictionary) is more relevant when dealing with non-fiction than with fiction. It would be challenging to continue this reflection with the case of a textual docufiction such as *Schindler's Ark* by Thomas Keneally (1982), a story midway between fiction and non-fiction. The term *faction* is even used for this work of literary journalism which is largely based on proven historical facts.

Without pursuing such linguistic considerations, Maurice Blanchot makes a similar observation to McCormick but in a more poetic tone:

> … the artist does not belong to truth because the work itself is what escapes the movement of the true. For always, whatever our perspective upon it, it revokes the true, eludes signification, designating that region where nothing subsists, where what takes place has nevertheless not taken place, where what begins over has never begun. It points into the realm of the most dangerous indecision, toward the confusion from which nothing emerges.[7]

This insistence on the notion of truth disallowed by fictional space has been well developed by literary theorists such as Tzvetan Todorov for whom "the sentences that make up the literary text are no more 'false' than they are 'real'. [...] the literary text is not subject to truth valuations; [...] it is neither true nor false but, specifically, fictional."[8] As I am constantly repeating to those of my students who are passionate about literature, the fictional literary text is the mode of being of the non-true, or the non-real—in contradistinction to the false, the fake, the counterfeit, or the untrue, all antithetical to authenticity and truth. It follows from this that the reader has no more of a mission to seek truths in the literary text than the novelist has to expound them.

Following Blanchot's conception of literary space, Danièle Sallenave, whom I take to be a professional reader,[9] says, "*by representing the world*, literature opens it to play, to dreaming, to utopia, to uchronia. When pitted against literature, the world ceases to be a place that reveals the true state of things: it becomes what it could or should be."[10] Because it is not reality, literature can freely explore the range of possibilities that our actual world does not permit. In other words, "novelists, in manufacturing their microcosms, offer us models of what is, and what could be, possible. Seeing fiction and reality as opposites thus loses its imperative."[11] Fiction offers us a *world of possibilities*—and here we come to the potentialities explored by the French experimental group known as OuLiPo—but in no case can it be a *possible world*. Fictional texts are outside "truth valuations" precisely because novelists create works of imagination: The shift toward the real is eschewed precisely because novelists weave their plots into stories, inevitably leading them to fabricate. In her study of the work of Maurice Blanchot, Daniela Hurezanu reminds us that in *L'imaginaire*, Jean-Paul Sartre discusses the imaginary "using the same words that Blanchot employs for literature. The imaginary is, like literature, a non-world, an escape-world which, as such, not only obviates our concerns in the actual world, but also allows us to 'elude *worldly* constrictions.'"[12]

For Blanchot the novel is:

> a work of bad faith, bad faith on the part of the novelist who believes in his characters and yet sees himself behind them, who does not know them, realizes them as unknowns, and finds in the language of which he is a master the means of manipulating them without ceasing to believe that they are escaping him. Bad faith of the reader who plays with the imaginary, who plays at being this hero that he is not, at taking for real what is fiction and finally lets itself be taken for that, and, in this enchantment that keeps existence at a distance, finds again a possibility of living the meaning of this existence.[13]

This is more or less what Umberto Eco is summarizing when he cites research by John Searle, echoing Blanchot: Such discourse has persisted since Coleridge's voluntary suspension of disbelief, articulated by Coleridge nearly two centuries ago.

> The reader has to know that what is being narrated is an imaginary story, but he must not therefore believe that the writer is telling lies. According to John Searle, the author simply pretends to be telling the truth. We accept the fictional agreement and we pretend that what is narrated has really taken place.[14]

All things considered, what is revealed by this bilateral contract (theoretically, the fictional pact), in which the writer deceives and the reader willingly accepts the deception, is the fundamental distinction between the "real world" and "narrative worlds," the former governed by "the principle of Truth," the latter ruled by "the principle of Trust."[15] Continuing his account in *Six Walks in the Fictional Woods*, Eco makes the following abstruse declaration:

> Apart from many important aesthetic reasons, I think that we read novels because they give us the comfortable sensation of living in worlds where the notion of truth is indisputable, while the actual world seems to be more of a treacherous place. This "alethic privilege" of fictional worlds also provides us with some parameters for challenging farfetched interpretations of literary texts.[16]

With its "alethic privilege," the novel cannot but seduce readers, if one agrees on what is meant by "alethic." To take this adjective in the sense with which Roland Barthes endows it in "What is criticism?,"[17] namely that "which is based on truth," we find a contradiction. If by that adjective, Eco suggests that the narrative worlds deliver statements that are true or false, possible or impossible, plausible or questionable according to the readers or the nature of the proposals, we again find ourselves far from the conviction according to which the literary work escapes the movement of the true. We may, however, discern in the fine grain of this phrase a reference to Todorov and his assumption that "the literary text is not subject to truth valuations, [...] it is neither true nor false but, specifically, fictional"[18]; indeed, a literary subject may be considered equally true or false to the extent that such considerations are alien to fiction. In another of his books, *Semiotics and Philosophy of Language* (1984), Umberto Eco notes that metaphor never tells the truth because it transgresses the structure of the real and proceeds to poetically reorder the world. By analogy, we could say exactly the same thing about the novel which, like metaphor, produces an image resulting from a linguistic construction.

This straining of the truth admittedly goes against the ethics of an historian, and whoever studies the historical novel realizes the rivalries and bitter disputes that make literature and historical accounts two exercises in style, each with their own characteristics. It would therefore be wise to conduct a major study of the historical novel and the quest for truth, examining the controversies that have vexed historians and novelists. In the same spirit, we would benefit from analyzing a number of identity disputes and literary frauds in order to determine if we should hold their perpetrators accountable for their distortions which are impediments to an alleged quest for truth; or if readers are guilty of putting words in the author's mouth by implicitly supporting the existence of an "alethic" dimension (in the sense that Barthes uses it) in the fictional space. Other questions would then arise: Does such dishonesty have consequences in the fictional space, or does it only cast a slur on the ethics of the writer? And the most important question: What do these deceptions manage to tell us about the status of fiction?

Illuminated by these considerations, we can see the incongruity for readers or writers wanting to embark on a quest for truth in a space that disallows it; hence, the convenient fact that no novelist can be blamed for being ignorant. From here, one need only take a small step before one is praising the *poietic* power (namely the creative capacity) of literature, a step blithely taken by Daniela Hurezanu when she concludes that "art and literature manage to come into existence, that is, manage to give *form* through the ability to control what had no form."[19] And perhaps, this is where we detect the imposture of literature which, by dint of mimicking the real, ends up by replacing it with a representation that dissimulates the inability of the real to compete with fiction. That said, I feel one should avoid extolling the *poietic* power of literature which partakes of a megalomaniac discourse. This discourse, which emanates more often from writers than professional readers, tends at once to glorify the almost divine powers of the creative capacity of fiction, and sounds like the revenge of the reader on a reality that provides too little satisfaction. Such idealization is all the more aberrant if one considers the decades of trumpeting about the decline of literature. How could literature wield so much power and yet also be at risk?

Since the notion of truth in the fictional space is so complex, it is reasonable to feel that the field of inquiry is ripe for development in new directions. But the difficult relationship that fiction has with the truth, or with the lack of truth, leads us via Peter McCormick to another reflection: How can a reader (obviously well aware of the theories of New Criticism) feel compassion when reading the adventures of fictional characters while being aware they are no more than paper beings? Exactly how can someone "be genuinely moved by sincerely believing in the existence of certain states of affairs he or she knows not to exist."[20] To these and many other questions, I hope to provide some answers in my final chapter.

Notes

1. See T. Todorov, *La notion de littérature* (Paris: Le Seuil, 1987), 86: "A fundamental trait of our civilisation is this concept of 'shadow-language', in perhaps changeable forms, but which are nevertheless the direct consequences of the objects they stand for ..."
2. R. Wellek & A. Warren, *Theory of Literature* (Melbourne: Penguin, 1966). 34.
3. M. Ouellette-Michalska, "Madeleine Monette, prix Robert-Cliche: Des doubles qui tournent bien", *Le Devoir*, 26 avril 1980, 23.
4. "1. a thing feigned or imaginatively invented, an invented statement, an untruth. 2. The action of feigning or of inventing imaginary events etc. (originally ... for the purposes of deception.)" *The New Shorter Oxford English Dictionary* (Oxford: Clarendon Press, 1993), Vol. 1, A-M, 941.
5. P.J. McCormick, "Fictions and Feelings", *Fictions, Philosophies and the Problems of Poetics* (Ithaca/London: Cornell UP, 1988), 138.
6. Ibid.
7. M. Blanchot, *The Space of Literature*, translated and introduced by Ann Smock (Lincoln: University of Nebraska Press, 1982 [1955]), 238.

8. T. Todorov, *La littérature en péril*, 13.
9. Danièle Sallenave is a French journalist and novelist who, in 1980, was the recipient of the Prix Renaudot, one of France's highest literary awards. She is also one of the 40 members of the Academie Francaise, the French state's advisory authority on the French language.
10. D. Sallenave, *Le don des morts* (Paris: Gallimard, 1991), 123.
11. B. Cannone, *L'écriture du désir*, 30–1.
12. J.-P. Sartre, *L'imaginaire* (Paris: Gallimard, 1940), 26, cited in D. Hurezanu, *Maurice Blanchot et la fin du mythe* (New Orleans: Presses Universitaires du Nouveau Monde, 2003), 105.
    It is the view of Hurezanu, a specialist in twentieth century French literature, that Sartre's imaginative world "is not only prone to Bovarysm [seeking solace in fantasies to escape daily life] but epitomizes our freedom, for it is the very essence of what is *possible*." (Herzanu's emphasis, 106).
13. M. Blanchot, *The Work of Fire*, translated by C. Mandell (Stanford: Stanford University Press, 1995), 192–193.
14. J. Searle, "The Logical Status of Fictional Discourse," *New Literary History* 14 (1975), cited in U. Eco, *Six Walks in the Fictional Woods*, (Cambridge, Mass. & London: Harvard University Press, 1994), 81.
15. U. Eco, *Six Walks in the Fictional Woods*, 75.
16. Ibid., 91.
17. R. Barthes, "What is criticism?" *Critical essays*, translated by Richard Howard (Evanston, Illinois: Northwestern University Press, 1972 [1964]), 255–260.
18. T. Todorov, *La littérature en péril*, 13.
19. D. Hurezanu, *Maurice Blanchot*, 204.
20. P.J. McCormick, *Fictions, Philosophies ...*, 132.

CHAPTER 9

Breaking New Ground: The Psycholiterary Approach to Fiction

Abstract How can the novel, devoid of real existence, generate real feelings in readers? The answer lies in a new approach: psycholiterary analysis. One of a range of multidisciplinary approaches, this articulates the osmosis occurring between the author's psyche and the reader's. Opting for an approach that takes aesthetic enjoyment into account, Vernay focuses on various philosophical positions, and on theories of the psyche. He also develops his argument about the role of emotions in literary interpretation, and about the conception and reception of the literary work. Finally, he integrates neuroscientific advances into his approach to analyze the behavior of "creators," and to reconcile the professional reader, attentive to various novelistic techniques, with amateur readers who abandon themselves more readily to the pleasure of the text.

Keywords Psycholiterary analysis • Psyche • Emotions • Literary interpretation • Pleasure of the text

> For the author, the main function of the literary work is to make something, not from nothing, but rather from the unexploited: to exhaust the affective potential and the share of imagination that have not been used in real life.
>
> —Didier Anzieu, *Créer Détruire*

I am of the strong view that the literary work is less concerned to express a sense of achievement per se, than to be an expression of the self. Let us return

© The Editor(s) (if applicable) and The Author(s) 2016

J.-F. Vernay, *The Seduction of Fiction*,
DOI 10.1007/978-3-319-39453-4_9

for a moment to Kundera, that great explorer of our inner selves, for whom "novels have always been concerned with the enigma of self. Once you create an imaginary being, a character, you are automatically faced with the question: What is the self? For how can the self be grasped? It is one of the fundamental questions forming the very basis of the novel."[1] This enigmatic borderland of the mind is the place depth psychology has long been exploring. And what is literature if not a meeting of two minds: That of the writer who produces the fiction, and that of the reader who consumes it.

> Reading a literary work is not simply the transfer from one mind to another of an organized complex of ideas and images, nor the active work of a subject on a collection of signs that he or she resuscitates in their own way from start to finish, it is also, throughout the entire length of an integrally planned journey, on the itinerary of which there is no means of changing even a comma; the reader welcoming someone: the designer and builder, who becomes the legal owner, acting as the host from beginning to end, and whose company cannot be dispensed with.[2]

So when I posit that psycholiterary analysis is a journey into the psyche of the creator, I mean that the exploration will be carried out as much in the author's psyche as in that of the reader who is also engaging in an act of creation. And since the interpretation of a literary text partakes of an attempt to understand the entire work, including the richness of its influences, I have good grounds for favoring a multidisciplinary approach.

"There are times in life when the question of knowing if one can think differently than one thinks, and perceive differently than one sees, is absolutely necessary if one is to go on looking and reflecting at all."[3] It is at the threshold of new research, and with these words of Michel Foucault in mind, that I have opted for a more personal approach to criticism, an admixture of my own sensitivity and of my affinities with philosophy, psychology, and psychoanalysis. I have termed it "psycholiterary analysis" and it is to this that I now turn my attention. From the outset, my approach arose from the family of explanatory critiques, and seems to have complex affiliations. This approach could be a distant relative of "esthopsychology" a term coined by Émile Hennequin (1859–1888) who advocated scientific criticism by seeing the literary work as a sign that releases an emotion, informing readers about the psychology of the creator, and claiming to be a social indicator. But even if psycholiterary analysis shares with esthopsychology some aesthetic, psychological, and sociological considerations, it does not share the tendency to adopt a scientific posture.

The author of *Histoire de la littérature française* (History of French literature), Gustave Lanson (1857–1934), who wished to shed light on the psychological and social dimensions of poetics, made it a point of honor to direct readers to the literary text, rather than to criticism. We shall soon see how Lanson's convictions have contemporary resonance, as I will detail below. As largely subjective trends in hermeneutic-inclined criticism,[4] psycholiterary analysis and Sartre-inspired criticism cover common ground in philosophy, psychoanalysis, and sociology. But the genealogy of my approach would not be complete without the essential contribution of reception theory, of which the theorists "Iser and Jauss situate their thinking within the German hermeneutic tradition. Both aim on the one hand to shift the hermeneutic questions of the text towards the dialogic relationship between text and reader, and on the other hand to conceive of this relationship as a properly historic process, taking into account social realities (of creation and reception)."[5]

My approach aims to reconcile professional readers, attentive to the various narrative techniques, and non-professional readers, who abandon themselves more readily to the pleasure of the text. The professional reader, who will conduct a psycholiterary analysis, will be invited to communicate the pleasure produced by the literary text, and to do justice to the flesh of words, proposing textual analyses which engage reflection as well as sensitivity.

Restoring Subjectivity to Favor

The restoring of subjectivity to favor will honor literature's quintessence which, for Barthes, "is that ensemble of objects and rules, techniques and works, whose function in the general economy of our society is precisely to institutionalize subjectivity."[6] Gustave Lanson had the courage to strongly oppose the scientific drift of literary criticism, and the honesty to admit the subjectivity of the individual, integrating it into his research ethics. According to him, "literature is not an object of knowledge: it is exercise, taste, pleasure. It is not known, nor learned: but practised, cultivated, loved."[7] In March 1984, in a debate with Gérard Genette, proponent of poetics, Marc Fumaroli followed in the steps of Gustave Lanson to denounce "the somewhat delusional pseudo-scientific approach of 'literary scholars' … [recalling] that there are two modes of knowledge of reality: literary knowledge, and scientific know-how." Considering an amalgam of these two modes, Fumaroli observed the impoverishment of literature by "second degree theoretical fictions," a decline which could be arrested by the "art of reading with discernment and of encouraging the reading of canonical texts."[8]

Since all artworks situate themselves within an ideology, the focus should be on the impact of the subjectivity of literary interpretation because of the capacity of the mind and of the emotions (which are consubstantial) to form or distort perceptions of reality. This is why I specify that my approach as a professional reader is part of a pedagogical project offering possible ways of reading. These elements sketch an outline of a partial (i.e. incomplete and biased) response which could be extended, refined, or abandoned. In no way does it intend to pin down the meaning of a work by presenting itself as the explanation that the authors themselves would have given, had they been asked to express their opinions on the topic.

Reading can also be conceived as the intersubjective relationship of a reader *in presentia*, and of an author *in absentia*, represented by words. In the logic of Iser's aesthetic of reception (*Rezeption-Aesthetik*), the interpretation of meaning is constructed in what the text reveals but also in what the reader (un)consciously wishes to grasp. The reader's receptive consciousness therefore ends up, according to Wolfgang Iser, by formulating the unformulated, without which the unformulated would be lost on the reader: "The production of the meaning of literary texts … does not merely entail the discovery of the unformulated, which can then be taken over by the active imagination of the reader; it also entails the possibility that we may formulate ourselves and so discover what had previously seemed to elude our consciousness."[9]

Consequently, the text is not so much read from outside as experienced from inside, all the more since it resonates with the sensitivity of the reader—sensitivity that the New Criticism sought to repress in order to objectify interpretation. It was thus convenient to repudiate any psychological dimension and to condemn the inclusion of the reader's emotional reaction which would be under the influence of an alleged affective fallacy.[10] And this is precisely what is challenged by psycholiterary analysis, since it seeks to factor in advances in cognitive science, to value the contribution of psychoanalysis which gives primacy to the unconscious, and to admit the plasticity of interpretation varying according to individual experience and to the "horizon of expectation" unique to each reader.

Factoring in Aesthetic Jouissance

It is not so long ago that the literary text was a pretext for the study of literary history: of diverse ideologies, concepts, and critical tools. It is to be hoped that the many theorists will change their minds, like Tzvetan Todorov in *La Littérature en péril* (2007), in order not to repeat the errors of the past which have produced such disinterest in literature. In his book *Petite Apologie de l'expérience esthétique* (brief apologia for aesthetic experience), Hans Robert Jauss ardently defends the thesis that "the attitude of jouissance, which art suggests and triggers, is the very basis of aesthetic experience; it is impossible to ignore this, and on the contrary we must take it as an object of theoretical reflection, if today we want to defend in the face of its detractors—well-read or otherwise—the social function of art and of the scientific disciplines at its service."[11] This clarion call to theorize aesthetic jouissance has perhaps not struck the imaginations of readers of *Toward an Aesthetic of Reception* but it is necessary to reflect on the aesthetic pleasure of fiction. Alain Vaillant concludes his *L'histoire litteraire* with a definition of literature which, according to him,

> designates all discursive productions of which the principal object, for the author and/or the reader, is pleasure born from the exercise of the imagination. This pleasure arises from specific cognitive mechanisms that set imagination in motion through language: imagination exercises in a specific way human mental and emotional faculties, and the consciousness of this intellectual activity is accompanied, whether the mental images be painful or happy, by euphoric sensations—as one can experience in sporting activity, at the very moment when pain is endured through effort. What we are labelling with the misnomer of aesthetic pleasure, produced by literature, is therefore nothing other than the jouissance born from this application of the imagination to the words—whatever the object and the nature of the words.[12]

What I find interesting is the dominating role that Vaillant attributes to the imagination and to the cognitive processes governing aesthetic jouissance. The "euphoric sensations" in question are the work "of a wizard brain, or a conjurer in us who decides at any moment what part of reality to use as the basis of our dreams, and to what extent our imagination must embellish reality, lighten it or fake it. This wizardry, second nature to us, has an adaptive role: giving minds the means to produce psychic pleasure", declares psychiatrist Roland Jouvent in his recent book written from a Darwinian perspective.[13]

Psycholiterary analysis is based on what proponents of cognitive science call "hot cognition"[14] (i.e., the emotional aspects of the brain's executive functioning) which shall not neglect the pleasure of the text nor theoretical reflection on it. In other words, my approach seeks to reconcile emotion and intellect, sense-experience and supra-sensitive knowledge (to borrow Platonic terms), and the impact of reception and its expression. As with any artwork whose aesthetic dimension has seduced, the intelligibility of the work ought to be brought to the fore so that it will be more appreciated and valued by others. Moreover, Jauss recalls that even Theodor Adorno—a staunch critic of aesthetic jouissance—finally admitted "the limit of all ascetic experience of art"[15] with the following thought: "But if jouissance was completely eliminated, one would no longer know how to answer the question, of what use is art?"[16]

Taking an Interest in the Variety of Philosophical Positions

Philosophical concerns about the novel (and more broadly about all that gives it its raison d'être: creation, words, and readers) which have motivated me from the beginning of my research have led me to read repeatedly and with delight philosophers such as Jean Baudrillard, Maurice Blanchot, Michel Foucault, Hans Robert Jauss, Plato, Clément Rosset, and Jean-Paul Sartre. In the wake of researchers like Camille Dumoulié, it is possible to honor "the necessary alliance of intellectuals and writers" (Philippe Sollers), by deepening the analysis of the relationship between literature and philosophy with other thinkers, such as Theodor Adorno, Gaston Bachelard, Alain Badiou, Gilles Deleuze, Jacques Derrida, Maurice Merleau-Ponty, Jean-Luc Nancy, Jacques Rancière, and Paul Ricoeur, to mention only a few.

With the psycholiterary approach, we cannot overlook the contribution of philosophy which embraces the psyche (understood as all mind-related phenomena). As Pierre Macherey aptly puts it, "When authors speak and write it is literature as such which is speculating as it establishes itself in the element of the philosophical, which exists prior to all individual philosophies."[17] The onus rests on literature, then, as Macherey announces, "to spell out the quintessential philosophical dimension of philosophy."[18] Discussing the proposition that Maurice Merleau-Ponty formulated in *The Prose of the World*, Camille Dumoulié observes that "the philosopher and the writer have the same relationship to truth: they build within their work and time an enigmatic universe for future centuries."[19] All these arguments advocate a closer kinship between literature and philosophy.

Wearing the dual hat of professor of philosophy and of English literature, Peter McCormick turns his philosopher's gaze on the role of the emotions in fiction. But in his book—*Fictions, Philosophies and the Problem of Poetics*—he unfortunately makes no distinction among the categories of readers (even though he recognizes a plurality by speaking of "communities of readers") when he inquires in the philosophical manner on the possible impact of the emotional involvement of fiction readers.[20] He opts for very abstract reasoning that overlooks both psychoanalysis and the advances in cognitive sciences (psychology, neuroscience, psycholinguistics, and affective science in particular), so we cannot expect to read here an explanation linked to concepts of empathy, or of transfer and projection. According to McCormick, belief does not come into play because readers are not responding to a narrative of events they know does not exist, but instead are reacting emotionally to the thought-contents expressed. No matter whether the literary text is truthful or not, the very nature of the representations—which are reflections of something—will suffice to arouse compassion in the reader. This is what Hans Robert Jauss identifies as "cathartic jouissance"[21] which, he says, "is also as much a release *of* something, as *for* something":[22] "The cathartic jouissance then plays—to quote Freud—the role of a lure (*Verlockungsprämie*) and can induce the reader or the viewer to assume standards of behaviour much more easily, and to show greater solidarity with a hero, as much in his exploits as in his sufferings".[23]

Peter McCormick has chosen as the point of departure for this view a passage from *The Unbearable Lightness of Being* by Kundera.[24] After positing that some readers might be affected by this extract, and mounting a long line of reasoning, he concludes: "How can such a fiction be called genuinely moving? Because some communities of readers come to feel a genuine grief that a leaving like Tereza's is virtually their own. In responding imaginatively to fiction we judge Tomas and ourselves, we feel for Tereza and ourselves."[25] But if this is the phenomenon of projection onto a female character in a fictional setting, would not it be necessary to construct a gendered theory that would only apply to a female readership? Could the male reader identify with a female character if the narrated situation touches the right chord? I raise this objection specifically, since the psychiatrist Alain Braconnier argues that it is incorrect to speak of genderless emotions since men and women "do not share the same affective culture."[26] He concludes his 1996 work *Le sexe des émotions* (Gendered emotions) by declaring that "if there are many feelings common to both sexes, science and experience show that in their affective life, men and woman sometimes differ considerably. Female emotions and male emotions can be in opposition. Ignoring these differences is often more dangerous than acknowledging them."[27] It seems to me that theoretically informed readers have everything to gain if they can synthesize the philosophical approach and observations from cognitive science and the humanities.

Drawing Lessons from Theories of the Psyche and Taking into Account Neuroscientific Developments

Psycholiterary analysis intends to question fiction's myth-making function by seeking to understand how the literary text structures itself in response to psychological mechanisms. Some theorists wanted to construct a psychoanalytic theory of creativity (or of the production of the work): Freud, Marie Bonaparte, Charles Mauron, Jean Bellemin-Noël, and Didier Anzieu, to mention only the most famous. Marie Bonaparte's psychobiography which emerged in the 1930s had shown its limits in its tendency to highlight and stigmatize personal failings of the author. In other words, the issue for the psychobiographer was to "grasp the unconscious motivations of the creative process" and "to recognize the deep interdependence which unites the authors' lives with their artistic production."[28] The text therefore used to become a pretext for medicalized discourse of literary analysis, seeing in the author's writings (those of Edgar Allan Poe, in this case) disturbing symptoms of a latent or manifest disorder. Three decades later, the psychocriticism of Charles Mauron was not much help either. In devoting themselves to the structural patterns of the text, to the repetition of motifs, to the "obsessive metaphors" (namely, "the unconscious nuclei that emerge from the texts"[29]), the critics thought they could penetrate the organization and the embodiment of the author's unconscious when, in search of the full picture, they were only unconsciously creating analytic templates.

In his 1996 book *La psychanalyse du texte litteraire* (*Psychoanalysis of the literary text*), Jean Bellemin-Noël defends the thesis that "every text is worked by unconscious forces that can be perceived and described."[30] He defined textanalysis in an earlier book as "the reconstruction of words of desire without reference, neither to one's knowledge of the author, nor to what we know from his other works, nor to the unbridled idiosyncrasy of the reader."[31] Textanalysis is a method that seeks no more to psychoanalyze the characters than the author. It simply proposes to "psychoanalyze texts" (Bellemin-Noël). "In short, the critic wants to embrace the 'fantasizing force' of the works analyzed, moving from the 'couch' where he reads to the 'armchair', where reading is 'reformulated': what remains of the original pleasure is to be found in the details of the analysis."[32] To be sure, Bellemin-Noël is not encouraging studies such as "The life and works of" this or that author, which has the disadvantage of orienting the literary analysis by way of random events and dramas that punctuate the author's life. In suggesting that his textanalysis avoids this pitfall, Bellemin-Noël by the same token rejects several factors: The possible influences that led the author to express himself on a particular subject, the richness that can be derived from an intertextual study, and the impact of the work on the reader; not to mention that his view strongly points to the suggestive power of psychoanalysis, a power which is responsible for its repeated indictments.

Ultimately, his textanalysis—it must be admitted—has many similarities to applied psychoanalysis and offers no safeguard against errors of misinterpretation. Moreover, his altogether poetic notion of "the text's unconscious" does not, correspond to any clinical reality, as pointed out by Didier Anzieu whose approach is much more legitimate. Like him, I am forging my own path

> ... between two hazards: that of traditional psychoanalysis which limits its investigation to the work's contents, situating it in relation to the author's suspected unconscious fantasies; and that of a semiotics which introduces psychoanalytic concepts, either approximate or diverted from their original meaning. I hear, for example, that it is language which produces the text or even that there would be an "unconscious of the text" distinct from those of the author and the reader. These premises are perhaps useful for linguists to pin down the indisputable effects of language on speech. But in my clinical practice, I have never encountered this unconscious, any more than this language.[33]

Except for the unconscious of the subject (whether author or reader), Anzieu is not ready to accept another, and common sense should align us to his opinion: "It is the unconscious of the author, a living and individual reality, which gives the text its life and singularity. And it is the reader's unconscious which, more than just encountering the life and singularity of the text, brings this new life, this originality. Deprived of these two unconsciousnesses, the text is a simple inanimate and anonymous entity, a body of dead letters."[34] What would be very useful as part of a psycho-literary approach is a psychoanalytic theory of aesthetics. I am aware that in his day, Freud had already identified this gap in his *Civilisation and its Discontents* (1929), and Anzieu contemplated elaborating such a theory in the foreword to his 1981 book *Le corps de l'œuvre* (*Body of work*); but, to my knowledge, this project has never come to fruition.

Books, being at once an author's intangible imagination and a reader's tangible object, could be conceived as a Winnicottian "transitional space" that Christine Arbisio-Lesourd defines as a "space of illusion where the internal and external worlds can coexist without contradiction."[35] Donald Winnicott said himself that this transitional space finds its extension in all areas which involve the twin aspects of creativity and imagination.

> Transitional objects and transitional phenomena belong to the realm of illusion which is at the basis of initiation of experience. This early stage in development is made possible by the mother's special capacity for making adaptation to the needs of her infant, thus allowing the infant the illusion that what the infant creates really exists.
>
> This intermediate area of experience, unchallenged in respect of its belonging to inner or external (shared) reality, constitutes the greater part of the infant's experience, and throughout life is retained in the intense experiencing that belongs to the arts and to religion and to imaginative living, and to creative scientific work.[36]

A space of fantasy from which emerges a sense of omnipotence, the novel seems to be an interface of reality that allows the writer to escape the limitations and the chores of everyday life. Wiser for these observations, the psycholiterary approach seeks to learn from theories of the psyche and see to what extent the professional reader can incorporate psychological and psychoanalytic models and concepts in his literary analysis to inform his co-readers. But there is more to it. The psycholiterary approach seeks also to assimilate advances in neuroscience in order to understand the interpretive work of the brain in the reading process. Recalling the tripartite brain proposed by Paul D. MacLean (the "triune brain"[37]), Roland Jouvent reminds us of the close association of the subcortex (otherwise known as the "horse" in MacLean's terminology, and which manages our emotions, needs, and senses), and the neocortex (the "rider"), which comments, transforms, elaborates, and interprets.

MacLean's "horse" "ensures the grounding in reality"[38] which allows the rider to "dream, to distract oneself, to do two things at a time, to day-dream when bored, to mess around by embellishing reality and transforming it into word play and imagination."[39] Jouvent also reminds us that psychoanalysis and behavioral therapies have much in common.

> In their own way, they each use brain plasticity to change attitudes and beliefs. We can say, schematically, that cognitive therapy tackles the direct control of emotional reactions while psychoanalysis bestowed on these reactions a time frame. This heterogeneity of different forms of psychotherapy should not forget that they all ultimately share the same goal: to restore to the wizard brain its natural aptitude to reshape the world, to make up stories and to utilize reality to produce psychic pleasure.[40]

Anyone wishing to ponder fiction's myth-making function, a feature that permits authors not to invent one type of reality, but to build an inner world entirely according to their own desires, should take an interest in the neocortex. Similarly, within the remit of the psycholiterary approach, professional readers will profitably inform themselves on the properties of the limbic system, the seat of affects. The contribution of neuroscience has enabled me to broaden the scope of my thoughts on the reception of literary works, confirming the fact that knowledge is bound up with affects. In his introduction, Joseph Forgas observes that

> The available research clearly points to a bidirectional rather than a unidirectional link between affects and cognition. There is much evidence for affects influencing attention, memory, thinking, associations and judgements … Equally, however, cognitive processes are integral to the elicitation of affective states, as people's appraisal of situational information activates appropriate emotional responses.[41]

Taking Affects into Consideration in the Interpretation, Creation, and Reception of Literary Work

To take affects into consideration in the interpretation of the literary work is to be interested in the investigations of affective science, a recent branch of the cognitive sciences that measures the impact of emotions on thought. These contributions will be invaluable in other respects for determining the role of emotions in the psychic activity of creators because they undoubtedly control them during the creative process. Joyce Carol Oates, always generous with good advice, once made the following recommendation: "To write, you have to have an emotional thread" and not let yourself be overwhelmed by research.[42] In this way, the writer uses his sensitivity to create, and the reader invests the work with affects, responding on an emotional level (with compassion, fear, sadness, pain, anger, passion, tenderness, sympathy, admiration, joy, enthusiasm, and so on) to the content of the story. In the same manner that sentimental literature (the sentimental or erotic novel, the sensational novel or "chick lit") as well as asentimental fiction like the grunge novel, thrives as much on the overflow of love as on the lack of it, the exploitation of fear is undergoing a resurgence among writers of thrillers, war novels, and dystopias and political novels, notably since the September 11 attacks in 2001.

Martha Nussbaum rightly states that "the emotions are not just likely responses to the content of many literary works; they are built into their very structure, as ways in which literary forms solicit attention."[43] It is possible, to give only one example among many, to compare paranoia and the literary construction of utopia. In his brilliant 1990 work titled *Utopie et primitivisme: Essai sur l'imaginaire anthropologique à l'âge classique* (Utopia and primitivism: on the anthropological imaginary in the classical age), Christian Marouby argues that "utopia is a structure of defence. It is the very reason why writers choose islands, for their natural protection. From the most objective realist perspective through to the deepest of our fantasies, from its geopolitically natural boundaries through to its matrix-like embrace of waters, insularity is reassuring."[44] And the author further declares:

> In its insularity, the utopian vision is characterized by perceiving an inner danger as coming from outside, against which the island is wholly structured. In the shelter of its inviolable borders, from the height of its inaccessible surrounds, it scans the horizon, waiting in anguish for the destruction which can only come from its self-generated tensions. It only recognizes its fantasies of mastery and domination in an imaginary external threat. So we must understand this insularity … as a space conducive to paranoia.[45]

Marouby articulates the notions of utopia and paranoia at the intersection of the fields of literature and psychoanalysis and perceives the closure of the classic utopian insular space as the result of a mechanism of defence in which the projection of fantasies plays a leading role. In analyzing the psychological mechanisms of projection in literary utopias, it would not be difficult to see how they are structured under the utopian impulse to appear in the guise of a silent tyranny by featuring ritualized lives, or tightly controlled communities like prisons. Therefore, while utopianism feeds on surplus, dystopia flourishes in saturation. Dystopia is thus not to be opposed to utopia as critics would have it (often presented as the polar opposite of utopia) since it is a projection of utopia—understood as a latent paranoia—on a continuum which peaks in the literary expression of a manifest psychotic mind.

Even before reading Martha Nussbaum, I understood that the affects also control literature at the level of reception, when reading a work, or listening to a play. How many writers admit to being more touched by the emotion their books generate in readers, rather than by praise of their elegant style? Sometimes, they even hope that the affects stirred by the text could bypass literary judgment. The representation of the affects in literature enjoys a space which is conducive to its thriving through language. But let us keep in mind that represented emotions are but literary constructs.

On the other hand, those feelings triggered within readers are certainly real. The novelist, and even more talented essayist, Belinda Cannone knows what she's talking about when she argues that "to make us experience their imaginary world, novelists build the illusion of presence, thereby arousing emotions."[46] I also closely align with Gustave Lanson when he posits that literary works are those "which, by the nature of their form, have the property to motivate in the reader imaginative expression, sentimental stimulation, and aesthetic emotions."[47] In his view, Lanson gives pride of place to the imagination, to the affects, and to aesthetics—a triad which in my view is inseparable from any art form.

In creating a novel, all techniques of verisimilitude—namely the creation of real-life characters, the inclusion of actual place names, and a plot that follows a linear and progressive chronology—refer to the reader's real world. This matching of spatiotemporal markers in the linguistic and extralinguistic domains is not just a safeguard against the bad habits of imagination, as it is conducive to the reader's immersion. Ultimately, these techniques are responsible for the non-professional reader's emotional involvement, an involvement which professional readers pride themselves on escaping when interpreting the work, due to their more analytical gaze. But can one escape the emotional involvement that fiction exerts on the various communities of readers when words are so charged with affect?

NOTES

1. M. Kundera, *L'art du roman* (1986), 39. The quotation is from the following interview with Kundera. "Milan Kundera on the art of the novel", in *Salmagundi Magazine*, http://salmagundimagazine.tumblr.com/post/64211845139/milan-kundera-on-the-art-of-the-novel. Accessed November 21st 2015.
2. J. Gracq, "En lisant en écrivant", *Œuvres complètes II* (Paris: Gallimard, 1995), 673.
3. M. Foucault, *The Use of Pleasure*, Vol. 2 of *The History of Sexuality*, translated by Robert Hurley (New York: Vintage Books, 1990), 8.
4. The branch of hermeneutic-inclined criticism (which includes theories derived from sociology, psychoanalysis, thematic criticism, and Ricoeur's phenomenology) is expounded by Thumerel, *La critique littéraire*, 150–67.
5. A. Vaillant, *L'histoire littéraire*, 195.
6. R. Barthes, *On Racine*, 172.
7. G. Lanson, *Histoire de la littérature française* (Paris: Hachette, 1894), cited in Thumerel, *La critique littéraire*, 75.
8. See J.-Y. Tadié, *La critique littéraire*, 273.
9. W. Iser, "The Reading Process: A Phenomenological Approach", *New Literary History* 3 (1972), cited in D. Lodge (ed.) *Modern Criticism and Theory: A Reader* (London/New York: Longman, 1988), 227.
10. See the writings of W.K. Wimsatt, in particular "The Affective Fallacy" in *The Verbal Icon: Studies in the Meaning of Poetry, with Two Preliminary Essays Written in Collaboration with Monroe C. Beadsley* (London: Methuen, 1970).
11. H.R. Jauss, *Toward an Aesthetic*, 137.
12. A. Vaillant, *L'histoire littéraire*, 358.
13. R. Jouvent, *Le cerveau magicien*, 9.
14. As opposed to "cold cognition" whereby human thought is endowed with rationality untarnished by affect.
15. T. Adorno, "Asthetische Theorie", in *Gesammelte Schriften* (t.VII, Francfort, 1970), 26–27. Cited in H.R. Jauss, *Toward an Aesthetic*, 139.
16. Ibid.
17. P. Macherey, *The Object of Literature* (Cambridge, UK: Cambridge University Press, 1995), 233.
18. Cited in C. Dumoulié, *Littérature et philosophie*, 100.
19. Ibid.
20. P.J. McCormick, *Fictions, Philosophies ...*, 131–151.
21. Michael Lacroix has rightly said that "Nowadays the meaning of the word 'catharsis' has changed because unlike our forebears, our contemporaries no longer consider emotion as poison, but as an asset. The cathartic activity that is encouraged in emotional therapies is intended to allow emotions to

manifest themselves not with the intention of getting rid of them, but rather to be fully enjoyed." M. Lacroix, *Le culte de l'émotion*, 68–9.

22. H.R. Jauss, *Toward an Aesthetic*, 162.
23. H.R. Jauss, *Toward an Aesthetic*, 137.
24. The scene in question is when Tomas realizes that Tereza has been searching through his papers and discovers love letters he has written to his mistress. But this only makes Tomas love Tereza all the more, even though she has violated his privacy.
25. P.J. McCormick, *Fictions, Philosophies ...*, 145.
26. A. Braconnier, *Le sexe des émotions* (Paris: Odile Jacob, 1996), 15. The psychiatrist further elaborates: "Positive emotions—joy, laughter, humor—usually occur in the same way and elicit identical reactions. [...] In contrast, negative emotions—anger, grief, guilt, and especially anxiety—are often a source of misunderstanding between men and women." 19.
27. A. Braconnier, *Le sexe des émotions*, 195.
28. Cited in J.-Y. Tadié, *La critique littéraire*, 152.
29. J. Bellemin-Noël, *La psychanalyse du texte littéraire* (Paris: Nathan, 1996), 63.
30. J. Bellemin-Noël, *La psychanalyse du texte littéraire*, 75.
31. J. Bellemin-Noël, *Vers l'inconscient du texte* (Paris: PUF, 1979), cited in *La psychanalyse du texte littéraire*, 75.
32. J.-Y. Tadié, *La critique littéraire*, 150.
33. D. Anzieu, *Le corps de l'œuvre*, 11.
34. Ibid., 12.
35. C. Arbisio-Lesourd, *L'enfant de la période de latence* (Paris: Dunod, 1997), 179.
36. D. Winnicott, *Playing and Reality*, with new preface by F. Robert Rodman (London and New York: Routledge, 2005), 19.
37. The triune brain consists of the reptilian brain of the paleo-mammalian accompanied brain (otherwise known as the limbic system) that form the subcortex crowning the neocortex (also called neomammalian brain).
38. R. Jouvent, *Le cerveau magicien*, 13.
39. Ibid., 61.
40. R. Jouvent, "Le cerveau, un cheval avec son cavalier", *Le point* 1915 (28 mai, 2009), 63.
41. J.P. Forgas (ed.), *Feeling and Thinking: the Role of Affect in Social Cognition* (Cambridge: CUP, 2001), 6.
42. Interview with Joyce Carol Oates, Academy of Achievement, http://www.achievement.org/autodoc/page/oat0int-3. Accessed November 21st 2015.
43. M. Nussbaum, *Poetic Justice: The Literary Imagination and the Public Life* (Boston: Beacon Press, 1995), 53.
44. C. Marouby, *Utopie et primitivisme. Essai sur l'imaginaire anthropologique à l'âge classique* (Paris: Seuil, 1990), 41.

45. And Christian Marouby adds in a footnote: "What indeed characterises paranoia is not so much the content of the fantasy (which can take a variety of forms) than the symptom formation process, aptly described by Freud as a projection: an unacceptable inner representation that is projected outside, so that the contents can then be seen as coming from outside, most frequently in the form of fantasies of aggression or persecution." Ibid., 45.
46. B. Cannone, *L'écriture du désir*, 50.
47. G. Lanson, *Essais de méthode, de critique et d'histoire littéraire* (Paris : Hachette, 1965), 396, cited in A. Vaillant, *L'histoire littéraire*, 86.

Conclusion

Abstract To conclude this plea for putting emotions back into literary interpretation, Vernay hopes that research will open new pathways to literary analysis, to which Anglo-Saxon cognitive criticism is already contributing. The French Ministry of Education has produced new curriculum outlines, acknowledging the role of the emotions. Despite an equal focus on cognition and emotions, one can point to the paradox of criticizing too-scientific literary theories while drawing on scientific advances. Yet the psycholiterary approach has the goal of shining new light on literature, especially the novel. In summary, this approach will value the unconscious, acknowledge the subjectivity of literary interpretation, examine aesthetic pleasure, and draw parallels with operational concepts of the psyche, seeking to determine the impact of the effects on both writer and reader.

Keywords Literary interpretation, Emotions, Cognitive criticism, Curriculum, Psycholiterary approach, Aesthetic pleasure

> Like philosophy and the humanities, literature is thought and knowledge of the social and psychic worlds in which we live. The reality that literature tries to comprehend is quite simply (but at the same time, nothing is more complex) human experience.
>
> —Tzvetan Todorov

© The Editor(s) (if applicable) and The Author(s) 2016

J.-F. Vernay, *The Seduction of Fiction*,
DOI 10.1007/978-3-319-39453-4

Concluding his book on the history of ideas, *Theory after theory* (2010), Nicholas Birns invites us to realize how important it is to offer fresh perspectives on the literary tradition, and in the same breath, he heralds the swan song of the age of theory. I hope to be more optimistic in wagering that French or international research will open up new pathways to literary analysis. Anglo-Saxon cognitive criticism contributes to this new impetus, having soared at the start of the twenty-first century with publications valuing the contribution of the emotions.[1] With this group of theorists, which include Sianne Ngai, Jane Thrailkill, Lisa Zunshine, Suzanne Keen, Patricia Ticineto Clough, and Jean O'Malley Halley, one could almost believe that only women are showing an interest in emotions!

Meanwhile, the French Ministry of Education, not to be left behind, finally acknowledged the impact of *pathos,* following its earlier endorsements of the technical complexity that underlies the art of fiction, and the singularity that constitutes the literary work. The latest benchmark statements defining the new curricula in French senior high schools from 30 September 2010 fully agreed with this development. Advocating a heightened sense of aesthetic awareness, the new benchmark statement does not disregard the crucial role of the emotions: "When dealing with the fictional world, one must not forget that the discovery of meaning occurs not only through the methodical analysis of the different identifiable aspects of the story (narrative and descriptive techniques in particular) but also by way of a personal relation to the text in which a reader's experience of emotion, pleasure or admiration plays a crucial role."

I would say it is all the more logical to focus equally on cognition and emotions since language and rhetoric, which constitute the core of the literary material, are able to convey either thoughts or feelings, if not both simultaneously. But if emotions are unique to each individual, can they be shared or passed on in the same way as knowledge? In other words, if a teacher enjoys reading the novels of, say, Henry James, is she nevertheless going to be able to share her love for a particular book? Nothing is less certain. The most that will happen is that the teacher's enthusiasm and personal style will ensure that the students enjoy the subject.

There is perhaps something paradoxical or ironic in, on the one hand, exposing the scientificity of certain literary theories and, on the other, in urging professional readers to take scientific advances into account in order to conceive new critical approaches. But the recognition of the plasticity and subjectivity of literary interpretation should act as an effective safeguard against treating literature as a science. Because to include science does not mean to mimic science. We must with good reason put an end to this literary culture in which literary erudition obscures feelings and the pleasure of reading. With psycholiterary analysis, I hope to be able to shine new light on the literary sphere as well as on the poetics of the novel.

To conclude this plea for a renewal of emotion in literature, I propose to summarize the defining features of psycholiterary analysis which, I hope, will win over a large audience. This approach—which aims at reconciling the professional reader with the non-professional, literature with the sciences, reason with emotions—will fulfill the following: It will value the notion of the unconscious, acknowledge the plasticity and subjectivity of literary interpretation, and examine aesthetic pleasure and the myth-making function of fiction (taking into account the roles played by the neocortex, the imagination, and cognitive processes); it will draw parallels with certain models and operational concepts of the psyche, and try to determine the impact of the affects (from the limbic system) in the inner workings of the creator (writer/reader) while making a clear distinction between the representation and the stirring of affects (i.e., emotional description versus emotional involvement); it will then merge the philosophical approach with scientific advances about our brain capacity, all this in order to understand the dynamics of the mind at the heart of writing which coalesces in a mirror-like desire—that of the writer reflecting that of the reader.

Note

1. See S. Ngai, *Ugly Feelings* (Cambridge, MA: Harvard University Press, 2005); S. Keen, *Empathy and the Novel* (New York: Oxford University Press, 2007); P. Clough & J. Halley, *The Affective Turn: Theorizing the Social* (Durham: Duke University Press, 2007); J. Thrailkill, *Affecting Fictions: Mind, Body, and Emotion in American Literary Realism* (Cambridge, MA: Harvard University Press, 2007); L. Zunshine, *Strange Concepts and the Stories They Make Possible: Cognition, Culture, Narrative* (Baltimore: Johns Hopkins University Press, 2008), among others.

Bibliography

Adorno, Theodor. 1970. *Asthetische Theorie*. Francfort: Gesammelte Schriften t.VII.
Angot, Christine. 2004. *Une partie du cœur*. Paris: Stock.
Anzieu, Didier. 1981. *Le corps de l'œuvre*. Paris: Gallimard.
Anzieu, Didier. 1996. *Créer, détruire*. Paris: Dunod.
Aragon, Louis. 1980. *Le mentir-vrai*. Paris: Gallimard.
Arbisio-Lesourd, Christine. 1997. *L'enfant de la période de latence*. Paris: Dunod.
Assoun, Paul-Laurent. 1997. *Psychanalyse*. Paris: PUF.
Auster, Paul, and Gérard de Cortanze. 1997. *La solitude du labyrinthe*. Paris: Actes Sud.
Baroni, Raphaël. 2015. Retrouver les émotions dans les études littéraires. *Vox Poetica*, February 2015. http://www.vox-poetica.org/entretiens/intVernay.html?fb_ref=Default. Accessed 10 Apr 2015.
Baroni, Raphaël, and Antonio Rodriguez (eds.). Les passions en littérature. De la théorie à l'enseignement. *Études de Lettres* no. 295, 2014/1.
Barthes, Roland. 1963. *Sur Racine*. Paris: Le Seuil.
Barthes, Roland. 1964. *Essais critiques*. Paris: Le Seuil.
Barthes, Roland. 1966. *Critique et vérité*. Paris: Le Seuil.
Barthes, Roland. 1972. *Critical Essays*. Trans. Richard Howard. Evanston, IL: Northwestern University Press.
Barthes, Roland. 1973. *Le plaisir du texte*. Paris: Le Seuil.
Barthes, Roland. 1975. *The Pleasure of the Text*. Trans. Richard Miller. New York: Hill and Wang.
Barthes, Roland. 1992. *On Racine*. Trans. Richard Howard. Berkeley and Los Angeles: University of California Press.

© The Editor(s) (if applicable) and The Author(s) 2016

J.-F. Vernay, *The Seduction of Fiction*,
DOI 10.1007/978-3-319-39453-4

Barthes, Roland. 2007/1966. *Criticism and Truth*. Trans. and ed. Katrine Pilcher Keuneman. NY and London: Continuum.

Baudrillard, Jean. 1979. *De la séduction*. Paris: Galilée.

Baudrillard, Jean. 1990. *Seduction*. Trans. Brian Singer. New York: St. Martin's Press.

Bayard, Pierre. 2007. *Comment parler des livres que l'on n'a pas lus*. Paris: Minuit.

Bayard, Pierre. 2007. *How to Talk About Books You Haven't Read*. Trans. Jeffrey Mehlman. London: Bloomsbury.

Bayard, Pierre. 2009. *Le plagiat par anticipation*. Paris: Minuit.

Bayard, Pierre, and Umberto Eco. Ce que lire veut dire. *Le Magazine Littéraire* 487(June 2009): 12–15.

Bellemin-Noël, Jean. 1996. *La psychanalyse du texte littéraire*. Paris: Nathan.

Benjamin, Walter. The Task of the Translator. In *Illuminations*, ed. and intro. Hannah Arendt. Trans. Harry Zorn. London: Random House.

Bessière, Jean (ed.). 1989. *Roman, réalités, réalismes*. Paris: PUF.

Birch, David. 1989. *Language, Literature and Critical Practice*. London/New York: Routledge.

Birns, Nicholas. 2010. *Theory After Theory: An Intellectual History of Literary Theory From 1950 to the Early 21st Century*. New York: Broadview.

Blair, John. 1979. *The Confidence Man in Modern Fiction*. London: Clarke, Doble & Brendon Ltd.

Blanchot, Maurice. 1955. *L'espace littéraire*. Paris: Gallimard.

Blanchot, Maurice. 1995. *The Work of Fire*. Trans. C. Mandell. Stanford: Stanford University Press.

Bloom, Harold. 1973. *The Anxiety of Influence: A Theory of Poetry*. Oxford: OUP.

Braconnier, Alain. 1996. *Le sexe des émotions*. Paris: Odile Jacob.

Cannone, Belinda. 2000. *L'écriture du désir*. Paris: Calmann-Levy.

Castano, Emanuele, and David Comer Kidd. 2013. Reading Literary Fiction Improves Theory of Mind. *Science*, 342(6156): 377–380.

Citton, Yves. 2007. *Lire, interpréter, actualiser. Pourquoi les études littéraires?* Paris: Editions Amsterdam.

Citton, Yves. 2010. *L'avenir des humanités. Economie de la connaissance ou cultures de l'interprétation?* Paris: La Découverte.

Clough, P., and J. Halley (eds.). 2007. *The Affective Turn: Theorizing the Social*. Durham: Duke University Press.

Coe, Jonathan. 1989. *A Touch of Love*. London: Penguin.

Coetzee, J.M. 2007. *Doubler le cap. Essais et entretiens*. Paris: Le Seuil.

Coleridge, Samuel Taylor. 1906 (1977). *Biographia Literaria*. London: Dent & Sons Ltd.

Compagnon, Antoine. 2007. *La littérature pour quoi faire?* Paris: Fayard/Collège de France.

Cordesse, Gérard, G. Lebas, and Y. Le Pellec. 1991. *Langages littéraires: textes d'anglais*. Toulouse: Presses Universitaires du Mirail.
Coulet, Henri (ed.). 1992. *Idées sur le roman. Textes critiques sur le roman français XXIIe–XXe siècle*. Paris: Larousse.
Damasio, Antonio. 1994. *Descartes' Error: Emotion, Reason and the Human Brain*. London & Basingstoke: Picador.
Damasio, Antonio. 1995. *L'erreur de Descartes: la raison des émotions*. Paris: Odile Jacob.
David, Jérôme. Chloroforme et signification: Pourquoi la littérature est-elle si soporifique à l'école? *Études de Lettres* 295, 2014/1. In *Les passions en littérature. De la théorie à l'enseignement*, eds. Raphaël Baroni and Antonio Rodriguez, 19–32.
Davis, Lydia. 2011. Some Notes on Translation and on Madame Bovary. *The Paris Review* 198(Fall): 88.
Deppman, Jed, Daniel Ferrer, and Michael Groden (eds.). 2004. *Genetic Criticism*. Philadelphia: University of Pennsylvania Press.
Derrida, J. 1978. *Of Grammatology*. Trans. Gayatri Chakravorty Spivak. Baltimore: Johns Hopkins Press.
Djikic, Maja, and Keith Oatley. 2014. The Art in Fiction: From Indirect Communication to Changes of the Self. *Psychology of Aesthetics, Creativity, and the Arts* 8(4): 498–505.
Dolto, Françoise. 1994. *Les étapes majeures de l' enfance*. Paris: Gallimard.
Dumoulié, Camille. 2002. *Littérature et philosophie*. Paris: Armand Colin.
Eagleton, Terry. 2012. *The Event of Literature*. New Haven/London: Yale University Press.
Eco, Umberto. 1965. *L'œuvre ouverte*. Paris: Le Seuil.
Eco, Umberto. 1979. *The Role of the Reader: Explorations in the Semiotics of Texts*, ed. Thomas Sebeok. Bloomington: Indiana University Press.
Eco, Umberto. 1979. *Lector in fabula, le rôle du lecteur*. Paris: Grasset.
Eco, Umberto. 1996. *Six promenades dans les bois du roman et d' ailleurs*. Paris: Grasset & Fasquelle.
Eco, Umberto. 1998. *Six Walks in the Fictional Woods*. Cambridge, MA: Harvard University Press.
Eco, Umberto. 2000. *On Literature*. Trans. Martin McLaughlin. NY: Harcourt.
Eco, Umberto. 2002. *De la littérature*. Paris: Grasset.
Ekman, P. 1982. *Emotion in the Human Face*. Paris: Maison des Sciences de l'Homme.
Eliot, T.S. 1965. *To Criticize the Critic and Other Writings*. London: Faber and Faber.
Felman, Shoshana. 1988. On Reading Poetry: Reflections on the Limits and Possibilities of Psychoanalytical Approaches. In *The Purloined Poe: Lacan,*

Derrida, and Psychoanalytic Reading, eds. Muller and Richardson. Baltimore, MD and London: Johns Hopkins University Press.
Finkielkraut, Alain. 1987. *La défaite de la pensée*. Paris: Gallimard.
Finkielkraut, Alain. 1995. *The Defeat of the Mind*. Trans. Judith Friedlander. NY: Columbia University Press.
Forgas, Joseph P. (ed.). 2000 (2001). *Feeling and Thinking: The Role of Affect in Social Cognition*. Cambridge: CUP/Maison des Sciences de l'Homme.
Foucault, Michel. 1984. *Histoire de la sexualité II: L'usage des plaisirs*. Paris: Gallimard.
Foucault, Michel. 1990. *The History of Sexuality, Vol. 2: The Use of Pleasure*. Trans. Robert Hurley. New York: Vintage Books.
Freud, Sigmund. 1933. *Essai de psychanalyse appliquée*. Paris: Gallimard.
Freud, Sigmund. 1989. Creative Writers and Day-Dreaming. In *The Freud Reader*, ed. Peter Gay. NY and London: Norton.
Genette, Gérard. 1982. *Palimpsestes. La littérature au second degré*. Paris: Le Seuil.
Genette, Gérard. 1991. *Fiction et diction*. Paris: Le Seuil.
Goleman, Daniel. 1996. *Emotional Intelligence: Why It Can Matter More Than IQ*. London: Bloomsbury.
Gracq, Julien. 1948. *André Breton*. Paris: José Corti.
Gracq, Julien. 1995. En lisant en écrivant. In *Œuvres complètes II*, 553–768. Paris: Gallimard.
Gutton, Philippe. 1973. *Le jeu chez l'enfant: essai psychanalytique*. Paris: Larousse.
Huguet, Michèle. 1987. *L'ennui ou la douleur du temps*. Paris: Masson.
Hurezanu, Daniela. 2003. *Maurice Blanchot et la fin du mythe*. New Orleans: Presses Universitaires du Nouveau Monde.
Hustvedt, Siri. 2012. *Living, Thinking, Looking: Essays*. London: Sceptre.
Iser, Wolfgang. 1972. The Reading Process: A Phenomenological Approach. *New Literary History* 3(2): 279–299.
Iser, Wolfgang. 1985. *L'acte de lecture. Théorie de l' effet esthétique*. Bruxelles: Mardaga.
James, Willliam. 1979. *Some Problems of Philosophy*. Cambridge, MA: Harvard University Press.
Jauss, Hans Robert. 1970. Literary History as a Challenge to Literary Theory. Trans. Elizabeth Benzinger. *New Literary History* 2(1): 7–37.
Jauss, Hans Robert. 1978. *Pour une esthétique de la réception*. Paris: Gallimard.
Jauss, Hans Robert. 1982. *Toward an Aesthetic of Reception*. Trans. Timothy Bahti. Minneapolis: University of Minnesota Press.
Jouve, Vincent. 2010. *Pourquoi étudier la littérature?* Paris: Armand Colin.
Jouvent, Roland. 2009. *Le cerveau magicien. De la réalité au plaisir psychique*. Paris: Odile Jacob.
Jouvent, Roland. 2009. Le cerveau, un cheval avec son cavalier. *Le point* 1915(28 May): 62–63.

Keen, Suzanne. 2007. *Empathy and the Novel.* New York: Oxford University Press.
Kristeva, Julia. 2000. *The Sense and Non-Sense of Revolt: The Powers and Limits of Psychoanalysis.* Trans. Jeanine Herman. New York: Columbia University Press.
Kundera, Milan. 1986. *L'art du roman.* Paris: Gallimard.
Kundera, Milan. 2005. *Le rideau: essai en sept parties.* Paris: Gallimard.
Kundera, Milan. 2007. *The Curtain: An Essay in Seven Parts.* Harper Perennial; Reprint edition.
Lacroix, Michel. 2001. *Le culte de l' émotion.* Paris: Flammarion.
Laplanche, Jean et J.-B. Pontalis. 1967. *Vocabulaire de la psychanalyse.* Paris: PUF.
LeDoux, Joseph. 1996. *The Emotional Brain: The Mysterious Underpinnings of Emotional Life.* New York: Simon & Schuster.
Lodge, David (ed.). 1988. *Modern Criticism and Theory: A Reader.* London/New York: Longman.
Macherey, Pierre. 1995. *The Object of Literature.* Cambridge, UK: Cambridge University Press.
Macherey, Pierre. 2013. *Philosopher avec la littérature: exercices de philosophie littéraire.* Paris: Hermann, coll. Fictions pensantes.
Maingueneau, Dominique. 2006. *Contre Saint-Proust. La fin de la littérature.* Paris: Belin.
Maisonneuve, Jean. 1985. *Les sentiments.* Paris: PUF.
Mannoni, Octave. 1969. *Clefs pour l'imaginaire ou l'autre scène.* Paris: Le Seuil.
Marouby, Christian. 1990. *Utopie et primitivisme. Essai sur l'imaginaire anthropologique à l'âge classique.* Paris: Seuil.
Marx, William. 2005. *L'Adieu à la littérature. Histoire d'une dévalorisation. XVIIIe–XXe siècle.* Paris: Les Editions de Minuit.
Maupassant, Guy de. 2006. "Le roman", préface to *Pierre et Jean*, 13–29. Paris: Pocket.
McCormick, Peter J. 1988. *Fictions, Philosophies and the Problems of Poetics.* Ithaca/London: Cornell UP.
Merleau-Ponty, Maurice. 1973. *The Prose of the World.* Evanston: Northwestern University Press.
Meyer, Catherine (ed.). 2005. *Le Livre noir de la psychanalyse.* Paris: Les arènes.
Millet, Richard. 2007. *Désenchantement de la littérature.* Paris: Gallimard.
Naccache, Lionel. 2010. La conscience révélée. *Philosophie magazine* 36(février 2010): 76.
Ngai, Sianne. 2005. *Ugly Feelings.* Cambridge, MA: Harvard University Press.
Nussbaum, Martha. 1995. *Poetic Justice: The Literary Imagination and the Public Life.* Boston: Beacon Press.
Nyssen, Hubert. 1997. *Éloge de la lecture* suivi de *Lecture d'Albert Cohen.* Montréal: Fides.
Oates, Joyce Carol. Writing and Reading the Emotional Thread. Interview on Academy of Achievement website: http://www.achievement.org/autodoc/page/oat0int-3. Accessed 21 Nov 2015.

Orr, Mary. 2003. *Intertextuality: Debates and Contexts.* Cambridge: Polity.
Ouellette-Michalska, Madeleine. 1980. Madeleine Monette, prix Robert-Cliche: Des doubles qui tournent bien. *Le Devoir* (26 April): 23.
OuLiPo. 1973. *La littérature potentielle.* Paris: Gallimard.
Pagès, Max. 1986. *Trace ou sens. Le système émotionnel.* Paris: Hommes et groupes.
Pennac, Daniel. 1992. *Comme un roman.* Paris: Gallimard.
Pennac, Daniel. 1994. *Reads Like a Novel.* Trans. Daniel Gunn. London: Quartet Books.
Raimond, Michel. 1987 (2000). *Le roman.* Paris: Armand Colin/HER.
Robert, Marthe. 1977. *Livre de lectures.* Paris: Grasset & Fasquelle.
Rose, Marilyn Gaddis. 1997. *Translation and Literary Criticism: Translation as Analysis.* Manchester UK: St. Jerome Publishers.
Rousset, Jean. 1961. *Forme et signification. Essai sur les structures littéraires de Corneille à Claudel.* Paris: José Corti.
Rushdie, Salman. 1996. *The Moor's Last Sigh.* London: Vintage.
Rycroft, Charles. 1985. *Psychoanalysis and Beyond.* London: Chatto & Windus.
Sallenave, Danièle. 1991. *Le don des morts.* Paris: Gallimard.
Sartre, Jean-Paul. 1940. *L'imaginaire.* Paris: Gallimard.
Sartre, Jean-Paul. 1948. *Qu'est-ce que la littérature?* Paris: Gallimard.
Sartre, Jean-Paul. 1965. *Esquisse d'une théorie des émotions.* Paris: Hermann.
Schaeffer, Jean-Marie. 2011. *Petite écologie des études littéraires. Pourquoi et comment étudier la littérature?* Paris: Thierry Marchaisse.
Scholes, Robert. 1979. *Fabulation and Metafiction.* Chicago: University of Illinois Press.
Searle, John. 1975. The Logical Status of Fictional Discourse. *New Literary History* 6(2), On Narrative and Narratives (Winter): 319–332.
Snow, C.P. 1959/1964. The Rede Lecture, 1959. In *The Two Cultures: And a Second Look.* Cambridge: Cambridge University Press.
Starobinski, Jean. 1978. Preface to H.R. Jauss, *Pour une esthétique de la réception.* Paris: Gallimard.
Steiner, George. 1996a. *Passions impunies.* Paris: Gallimard.
Steiner, George. 1996b. *No Passion Spent: Essays 1978–1996.* London and Boston: Faber and Faber.
Tadié, Jean-Yves. 1987. *La critique littéraire au XX e siècle.* Paris: Belfond.
Taylor, Jane M. 2001. *The Poetry of François Villon: Text and Context.* Cambridge, UK: Cambridge University Press.
Thrailkill, Jane F. 2007. *Affecting Fictions: Mind, Body, and Emotion in American Literary Realism.* Cambridge, MA: Harvard University Press.
Thumerel, Fabrice. 2002. *La critique littéraire.* Paris: Armand Colin.
Todorov, Tzvetan. 1987. *La notion de littérature.* Paris: Le Seuil.
Todorov, Tzvetan. 2007. *La littérature en péril.* Paris: Flammarion.
Vaillant, Alain. 2010. *L'histoire littéraire.* Paris: Armand Colin.

Valéry, Paul. 1943. *Tel quel*. Paris: Gallimard.

Vernay, Jean-François. 2007. *Water from the Moon: Illusion and Reality in the Works of Australian Novelist Christopher Koch*. NY: Cambria Press.

Vernay, Jean-François. 2014. The Truth About Fiction as Possible Worlds. *Journal of Language, Literature and Culture* 61(2): 133–141.

Vincent, Jean-Didier. 1986. *Biologie des passions*. Paris: Odile Jacob.

Wall, Irwin. 2001. The Mentir-vrai and Aragon's Politics. *The Romantic Review* 92(1/2).

Wellek, René, and Austin Warren. 1966. *Theory of Literature*. Melbourne: Penguin.

Wellek, René, and Austin Warren. 1971. *La théorie littéraire*. Paris: Le Seuil.

Williams, Linda Ruth. 1995. *Critical Desire: Psychoanalysis and the Literary Subject*. London: Edward Arnold.

Wimsatt, W.K. 1970. *The Verbal Icon: Studies in the Meaning of Poetry, with Two Preliminary Essays Written in Collaboration with Monroe C. Beadsley*. London: Methuen.

Winnicott, Donald. 1971 (2002). *Jeu et réalité: l'espace potentiel*. Trans. Claude Monod and J.-B. Pontalis. Paris: Gallimard.

Winnicott, Donald. 2005. *Playing and Reality*. With new preface by F. Robert Rodman. London and New York: Routledge.

Zunshine, Lisa 2008. *Strange Concepts and the Stories They Make Possible: Cognition, Culture, Narrative*. Baltimore: Johns Hopkins University Press.

Index

Note: Page numbers with "n" denote notes

© The Editor(s) (if applicable) and The Author(s) 2016
J.-F. Vernay, *The Seduction of Fiction*,
DOI 10.1007/978-3-319-39453-4

The manufacturer's authorised representative in the EU is Springer Nature Customer Service Centre GmbH, Europaplatz 3, 69115 Heidelberg, Germany. If you have any concerns regarding our products, please contact ProductSafety@springernature.com

Printed and bound by CPI Group (UK) Ltd, Croydon, CR0 4YY
01/10/2026
02225978-0003